O'Hurley's Return

Skin Deep

Also by Nora Roberts
in Large Print:

Carolina Moon
Considering Kate
Cordina's Crown Jewel
Dance of Dreams
Dance Upon the Air
Dual Image
Enchanted
Heart of the Sea
Heaven and Earth
Irish Hearts
Irish Rebel
Jewels of the Sun
Midnight Bayou
Mind Over Matter
Night Shield

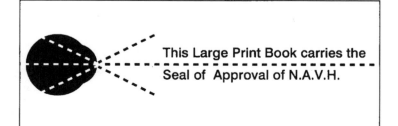

This Large Print Book carries the
Seal of Approval of N.A.V.H.

O'Hurley's Return

Skin Deep

Nora Roberts

Thorndike Press • Waterville, Maine

Published in 2005 by arrangement with Harlequin Books S.A.

Thorndike Press® Large Print Romance.

The tree indicium is a trademark of Thorndike Press.

The text of this Large Print edition is unabridged. Other aspects of the book may vary from the original edition.

Set in 16 pt. Plantin by Al Chase.

Printed in the United States on permanent paper.

Library of Congress Cataloging-in-Publication Data

Roberts, Nora.
    O'Hurley's return : skin deep. Book one / by Nora Roberts.
        p. cm. — (Thorndike Press large print romance)
    ISBN 0-7862-7636-3 (lg. print : hc : alk. paper)
    1. Large type books. I. Title. II. Thorndike Press large print romance series.
PS3568.O243O368 2005
    813′.54—dc22   2005018178

To my sisters,
Mary Anne, Carol, Bobbi, Carolyn,
Maxine, Reba, Barbara and Joyce,
all of whom I've been lucky enough
to inherit through marriage.

As the Founder/CEO of NAVH, the only national health agency solely devoted to those who, although not totally blind, have an eye disease which could lead to serious visual impairment, I am pleased to recognize Thorndike Press★ as one of the leading publishers in the large print field.

Founded in 1954 in San Francisco to prepare large print textbooks for partially seeing children, NAVH became the pioneer and standard setting agency in the preparation of large type.

Today, those publishers who meet our standards carry the prestigious "Seal of Approval" indicating high quality large print. We are delighted that Thorndike Press is one of the publishers whose titles meet these standards. We are also pleased to recognize the significant contribution Thorndike Press is making in this important and growing field.

Lorraine H. Marchi, L.H.D.
Founder/CEO
NAVH

★ Thorndike Press encompasses the following imprints: Thorndike, Wheeler, Walker and Large Print Press.

THE O'HURLEYS!

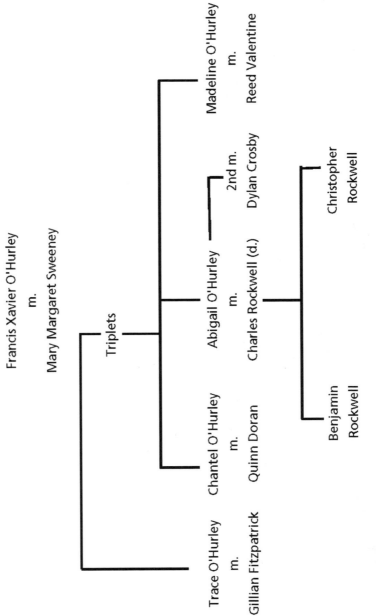

Francis Xavier O'Hurley
m.
Mary Margaret Sweeney

Triplets

Trace O'Hurley
m.
Gillian Fitzpatrick

Chantel O'Hurley
m.
Quinn Doran

Abigail O'Hurley
m.
Charles Rockwell (d.)

2nd m.
Dylan Crosby

Madeline O'Hurley
m.
Reed Valentine

Benjamin
Rockwell

Christopher
Rockwell

Prologue

"I don't know what we're going to do with that girl."

"Now, Molly." With his eye on the mirror, Frank O'Hurley added a touch of pancake makeup to his chin to make certain his face didn't shine onstage. "You worry too much."

"Worry?" As she twisted to pull the zipper up the back of her dress, Molly remained at the dressing room door so that she could watch the corridor backstage. "Frank, we have four children and I love every one of them, but Chantel's middle name is trouble."

"You're too hard on the girl."

"Because you're not hard enough."

Frank chuckled, then turned around to scoop his wife into his arms. More than twenty years of marriage hadn't dulled his feelings for her a whit. She was still his Molly, pretty and bright, even though she was the mother of his twenty-year-old son and his three teenage daughters. "Molly, my love, Chantel's a beautiful young girl."

"And she knows it." Molly peeked over Frank's shoulder at the backstage door, willing it to open. Where was that girl? They had fifteen minutes before they were due onstage, and Chantel had yet to make an appearance.

When she had given birth to her three daughters, each within minutes of the next, she hadn't known that the first one would give her more to worry about than the other two combined.

"It's her looks that are going to get her in trouble," Molly muttered. "When a girl looks like Chantel, boys are bound to come sniffing around."

"She can handle the boys."

"Maybe that worries me, too. She handles them too well." How could she expect a man as simple and kindhearted as her Frank to understand the complexities of women? Instead, she fell back on an old standard. "She's only sixteen, Frank."

"And how old were you when you and I — ?"

"That was different," Molly said, but she was forced to laugh at the grin Frank sent her. "Well, it was." She straightened his tie, then brushed powder from his lapels as she spoke. "She might not have the good fortune to meet a man like you."

Cupping his hands under her elbows, he held her still. "What kind of man is that?"

With her hands on his shoulders, she looked at his face. It was thin, and already lined, but the eyes were the eyes of the smooth-talking boy she'd lost her head over. Though he'd never quite come up with that moon on a silver platter that he'd once promised her, they were partners in every sense of the word. For better or worse — through thick and thin. There had been a lot of thin. She'd spent more than half of her life with the man, Molly thought, and he could still charm her.

"A dear one," she told him, and brought her lips to his.

At the sound of the back door closing, Molly pulled away. "Now don't jump on her, Molly," Frank began as he caught his wife's arm. "You know it'll just put her back up, and she's here now."

Grumbling, Molly drew away as Chantel danced down the corridor. She was wearing a vivid red sweater and snug black slacks that showed off her blooming young shape. The brisk fall air had whipped color into her cheeks, highlighting already elegant bones. Her eyes were a deep, deep blue and held a breezy, self-satisfied expression.

"Chantel."

With her natural flair for drama and timing, Chantel paused outside the door of the dressing room she shared with her sisters. "Mom." Her lips turned up at the corners, and the smile spread farther when she saw her father wink at her over Molly's shoulder. She knew she could always count on Pop. "I know I'm a little late, but I'll be ready. I had the most wonderful time." Excitement added spark to beauty. "Michael let me drive his car."

"That fancy little red number — ?" Frank began. Then he coughed into his hand as Molly leveled him with a look.

"Chantel, you've only had your license a few weeks." How she hated to lecture, Molly thought as she wound herself up for it. She knew what it was to be sixteen, and because of that she knew there was no way around what she had to do. "Your father and I don't think you're ready to drive unless one of us is with you. And in any case," she continued before Chantel could get out her first protest, "it isn't smart to get behind the wheel of someone else's car."

"We were on the back roads." Chantel came over and kissed her mother on both cheeks. "Don't worry so much. I have to have some fun or I'll just shrivel up."

Molly recognized the ploy too well, and

she stood firm. "Chantel, you're too young to go off in some boy's car."

"Michael's not a boy. He's twenty-one."

"That only makes my point."

"He's a creep." Trace announced calmly as he came into the corridor. He only lifted a brow when Chantel turned on him, eyes flashing. "And if I find out he's touched you I'll rip his face off."

"It's none of your business," Chantel told him. It was one thing to be lectured by her mother, quite another to hear it from her brother. "I'm sixteen, not six, and I'm sick and tired of being hovered over."

"Too bad." He took her chin in his hand, holding it steady when she tried to jerk away. He had a rougher, masculine version of Chantel's beauty. Looking at them, Frank felt pride swell in him until he thought he was going to burst. They were the fire-eaters of the family, more like their mother than him. He loved them with all his heart.

"All right now, all right." Playing peacemaker, he stepped up. "We'll get into all this business later. Right now, Chantel has to change. Ten minutes, princess," he murmured. "Don't dawdle. Come on, Molly, let's go warm up the crowd."

Molly sent Chantel a quiet look that

warned her the business wasn't over, then softened and touched her daughter's cheek. "We've a right to worry about you, you know."

"Maybe." Chantel's chin was still high. "But you don't need to. I can take care of myself."

"I'm afraid you can." With a little sigh, she walked with her husband down toward the small stage where they would earn their living for the rest of the week.

Far from mollified, Chantel put her hand on the knob of the door behind her before she faced her brother. "I decide who touches me, Trace. Remember that."

"Just make sure your friend with the fancy car behaves himself. Unless you'd like both his arms broken."

"Oh, go to hell."

"Probably will," he said easily. Then he tugged her hair. "I'll be clearing a path for you, little sister."

Because she wanted to laugh, Chantel yanked open the door, then shut it in his face.

Maddy glanced over as she buttoned the back of Abby's costume. "So, you decided to show up."

"Don't you start." Moving quickly, Chantel pulled a dress that matched her sisters' off an iron bar that spanned the width of the room.

"Wouldn't dream of it. Sounded interesting out in the hall, though."

"I wish they'd stop fussing over me." Chantel tossed the dress down, then peeled off her sweater. The skin below was pale and smooth, the curves already soft and feminine.

"Look at it this way," Maddy said as she finished Abby's buttons. "They're so busy fussing at you, they hardly ever pick on Abby and me."

"You owe me." Chantel slipped out of her slacks with brisk movements and stood in bra and panties.

"Mom really was worried," Abby interjected. Since her own makeup and hair were finished, she arranged the tubes and pots that would set Chantel's face for the stage.

Feeling a little pang of guilt, Chantel plopped down in front of the mirror the three of them shared. "She didn't have to be. I was fine. I had fun."

"Did he really let you drive his car?" Interested, Maddy picked up a brush to fix Chantel's hair.

"Yeah. It felt . . . I don't know, it felt important." She glanced around the cramped, windowless room with its concrete floor and

15

dingy walls. "I'm not always going to be in a dump like this, you know."

"Now you sound like Pop." With a smile, Abby handed her a makeup sponge.

"Well, I'm not." With years of experience already behind her, Chantel added the color to her face in quick strokes. "One day I'm going to have a dressing room three times this big. All white, with carpet so thick you'll sink up to your ankles."

"I'd rather have color," Maddy said, dreaming herself for a moment. "Lots and lots of color."

"White," Chantel repeated firmly. Then she stood to put on her dress. "And it's going to have a star on the door. I'm going to ride in a limo and have a sports car that makes Michael's look like a toy." Her eyes darkened as she pulled on the dress, which had been mended too many times to count. "And a house with acres of garden and a big stone pool."

Because dreams were part of their heritage, Abby elaborated as she did up Chantel's buttons. "When you walk into a restaurant, the maître d' will recognize you and give you the best table and a bottle of champagne on the house."

"You'll be gracious to photographers," Maddy went on, handing Chantel her earrings. "And never refuse an autograph."

"Naturally." Enjoying herself, Chantel clipped the glass stones at her ears, thinking of diamonds. "There'll be two enormous suites in the house for each of my sisters. We'll sit up at night and eat caviar."

"Make it pizza," Maddy instructed, resting an elbow on her shoulder.

"Pizza *and* caviar," Abby put in, then stood on the other side.

With a laugh, Chantel slipped her arms around her sisters' waists. They were a unit now, just as they had been in the womb. "We're going to go places. We're going to be somebody."

"We already are." Abby tilted her head to look at Chantel. "The O'Hurley Triplets."

Chantel looked at the reflection the mirror tossed back. "And nobody's ever going to forget it."

Chapter One

The house was big and cool and white. In the early-morning hours, a breeze came through the terrace doors Chantel had left unlatched, bringing in the scents of the garden. Across the lawn, hidden from the main house by trees, was a gazebo, painted white, with wisteria climbing up the trellises. Sometimes, when the wind was right, Chantel could catch the perfume from her bedroom window.

On the east side of the lawn was an elaborate marble fountain. It was quiet now. She rarely had it turned on when she was alone. Near it was the pool, an octagonal stone affair skirted by a wide patio and flanked by another, smaller, white house. There was a tennis court beyond a grove of trees, but it had been weeks since she'd had the time or the inclination to pick up a racket.

Surrounding the estate was a stone fence, twice as tall as a man, that alternately gave her a sense of security or the feeling of being hemmed in. Still, inside the house, with its

18

lofty ceilings and cool white walls, she often forgot about the fence and the security system and the electronic gate; it was the price she paid for the fame she had always wanted.

The servants' quarters were in the west wing, on the first floor. No one stirred there now. It was barely dawn, and she was alone. There were times Chantel preferred it that way.

As she bundled her hair under a hat, she didn't bother to check the results in the three foot mirror in her dressing room. The long shirt and flat-heeled shoes she wore were chosen for comfort, not for elegance. The face that had broken men's hearts and stirred women's envy was left untouched by cosmetics. Chantel protected it by pulling down the brim of her hat and slipping on enormous sunglasses. As she picked up the bag that held everything she thought she would need for the day, the intercom beside the door buzzed.

She checked her watch. Five forty-five. Then she pushed the button. "Right on time."

"Good morning, Miss O'Hurley."

"Good morning, Robert. I'll be right down." After flipping the switch that released the front gate, Chantel started down the wide double staircase that led to the main floor. The mahogany rail felt like satin under her fingers as she trailed them down. Overhead, a chandelier hung, its prisms quiet in the dim light. The marble floor shone like glass. The house was a suitable showcase for the star she had worked to become. Chantel had yet to take any of it for granted. It was a dream that had rolled from, then into, other dreams, and it took time and effort and skill to maintain. But then she'd been working all her life and felt entitled to the benefits she had begun to reap.

As she walked to the front door, the phone began to ring.

Damn it, had they changed the call on her? Because she was up and the servants weren't, Chantel crossed the hall to the library and lifted the receiver. "Hello." Automatically she picked up a pen and prepared to make a note.

"I wish I could see you right now." The familiar whisper had her palms going damp, and the pen slipped out of her hand and fell soundlessly on the fresh blotter. "Why did you change your number? You're not afraid of me, are you? You mustn't be afraid of me, Chantel. I won't hurt you. I just want to touch you. Just touch you. Are you getting dressed? Are you —"

20

With a cry of despair, Chantel slammed down the receiver. The sound of her breathing in the big, empty house seemed to echo back to her. It was starting again.

Minutes later, her driver noticed only that she didn't give him the easy, flirtatious smile she usually greeted him with before she climbed into the back of the limo. Once inside, Chantel tipped her head back, closed her eyes and willed herself to calm. She had to face the camera in a few hours and give it her best. That was her job. That was her life. Nothing could be allowed to interfere with that, not even the fear of a whisper over the phone or an anonymous letter.

By the time the limo passed through the studio gates, Chantel had herself under control again. She should be safe here, shouldn't she? Here she could pour herself into the work that still fascinated her. Inside the dozens of big domed buildings, magic happened, and she was part of it. Even the ugliness was just pretend. Murder, mayhem and passion could all be simulated. Fantasyland, her sister Maddy called it, and that was true enough. But, Chantel thought with a smile, you had to work your tail off to make the fantasy real.

She was sitting in makeup at six-thirty

and having her hair fussed over and styled by seven. They were in the first week of shooting, and everything seemed fresh and new. Chantel read over her lines while the stylist arranged her hair into the flowing silver-blond mane her character would wear that day.

"Such incredible bulk," the stylist murmured as she aimed the hand-held dryer. "I know women who would sell their blue-chip stocks for hair as thick as this. And the color!" She bent down to eye level to look in the mirror at the results of her work. "Even I have a hard time believing it's natural."

"My grandmother on my father's side." Chantel turned her head a bit to check her left profile. "I'm supposed to be twenty in this scene, Margo. Am I going to pull it off?"

With a laugh, the stringy redhead stood back. "That's the least of your worries. It's a shame they're going to dump rain all over this." She gave Chantel's hair a final fluff.

"You're telling me." Chantel stood when the bib was removed. "Thanks, Margo." Before she'd taken two steps, her assistant was at her elbow. Chantel had hired him because he was young and eager and had no ambitions to be an actor. "Are you going to crack the whip, Larry?"

Larry Washington flushed and stuttered,

22

as he always did during his first five minutes around Chantel. He was short and well built, fresh out of college, and had a mind that soaked up details. His biggest ambition at the moment was to own a Mercedes. "Oh, you know I'd never do that, Miss O'Hurley."

Chantel patted his shoulder, making his blood pressure soar. "Somebody has to. Larry, I'd appreciate it if you'd scout up the assistant director and tell him I'm in my trailer. I'm going to hide out there until they're ready to rehearse." Her co-star came into view carrying a cigarette and what Chantel accurately gauged to be a filthy hangover.

"Would you like me to bring you some coffee, Miss O'Hurley?" As he asked, Larry shifted to distance himself. Everyone with brains had quickly figured out that it was best to avoid Sean Carter when he was dealing with the morning after.

"Yes, thanks." Chantel nodded to a few members of the crew as they tightened up the works on the first set, a train station, complete with tracks, passenger cars and a depot. She'd say her desperate goodbyes to her lover there. She could only hope he'd gotten his headache under control by then.

Larry kept pace with her as she crossed

the set, walking under lights and around cables. "I wanted to remind you about your interview this afternoon. The reporter from *Star Gaze* is due here at twelve-thirty. Dean from publicity said he'd sit in with you if you wanted."

"No, that's all right. I can handle a reporter. See if you can get some fresh fruit, sandwiches, coffee. No, make that iced tea. I'll do the interview in my dressing room."

"All right, Miss O'Hurley." Earnestly he began to note it down in his book. "Is there anything else?"

She paused at the door of her dressing room. "How long have you been working for me now, Larry?"

"Ah, just over three months, Miss O'Hurley."

"I think you could start to call me Chantel." She smiled, then closed the door on his astonished pleasure.

The trailer had been recently redecorated for her taste and comfort. With the script still in her hand, Chantel walked through the sitting room and into the small dressing area beyond. Knowing her time was limited, she didn't waste it. After stripping out of her own clothes, she changed into the jeans and sweater she would wear for the first scene.

She was to be twenty, a struggling art student on the down slide of her first affair. Chantel glanced at the script again. It was good, solid. The part she'd gotten would give her an opportunity to express a range of feeling that would stretch her creative talents. It was a challenge, and all she had to do was take advantage of it. And she would. Chantel promised herself she would.

When she had read *Strangers* she'd cast herself in the part of Hailey, the young artist betrayed by one man, haunted by another; a woman who ultimately finds success and loses love. Chantel understood Hailey. She understood betrayal. And, she thought as she glanced around the elegant little room again, she understood success and the price that had to be paid for it.

Though she knew her lines cold, she kept the script with her as she went back to the sitting room. With luck she would have time for one quick cup of coffee before they ran through the scene. When she was working on a film, Chantel found it easy to live off coffee, a quick, light lunch and more coffee. The part fed her. There was rarely time for shopping, a dip in the pool or a massage at the club until a film was wrapped. Those were rewards for a job well done.

She started to sit, but a vase of vivid red roses caught her eye. From one of the studio heads, she thought as she walked over to pick up the card. When she opened it, the script slid out of her hand and onto the floor. "I'm watching you always. Always."

At the knock on her door, she jerked back, stumbling against the counter. The scent of the roses at her back spread, heady and sweet. With a hand to her throat, she stared at the door with the first real fear she'd ever experienced.

"Miss O'Hurley . . . Chantel, it's Larry. I have your coffee."

With a breathless sob, she ran across the room and jerked open the door. "Larry —"

"It's black the way you — What's wrong?"

"I — I just —" She cut herself off. Control, she thought desperately. You lose everything if you lose control. "Larry, do you know anything about these flowers?" She gestured back, but couldn't look at them.

"The roses. Oh, one of the caterers found them while she was setting up breakfast. Since they had your name on them, I went ahead and put them in here. I know how much you like roses."

"Get rid of them."

"But —"

"Please." She stepped out of the dressing room. People. She wanted lots of people around her. "Just get rid of them, Larry."

"Sure." He stared at her back as she walked toward the set. "Right away."

Four aspirin and three cups of coffee had brought Sean Carter back to life. It was time to work, and nothing could be allowed to interfere with that — not a hangover, not a few frightening words printed on a card. Chantel had worked hard to project an image of glamour and style. She'd worked just as hard not to develop a reputation as a temperamental actress. She was ready when called and always knew her lines. If a scene took ten hours to shoot, then it took ten hours. She reminded herself of all of this as she approached Sean and their director.

"How come you always look as though you stepped out of the pages of a fashion magazine?" Sean grumbled, but Chantel observed that makeup had dealt with the shadows under his eyes. His skin was tanned and shaved smooth. His thick, mahogany-colored hair was styled casually, falling across his brow. He looked young, healthy and handsome, the dream lover for an idealistic girl.

Chantel lifted a hand and let it rest on his cheek. "Because, darling, I did."

"What a woman." Because the aspirin had made him feel human again, Sean grabbed Chantel and leaned her back in a dramatic dip. "Let me ask you this, Rothschild," he said, calling to the director while his lips hovered inches from Chantel's. "How could a man in his right mind leave a woman like this?"

"It hasn't been established that you — or Brad," Mary Rothschild corrected, referring to the role, "is in his right mind."

"And you're such a cad," Chantel reminded Sean.

Pleased to remember it, Sean brought her up again. "I haven't played a real cad in about five years. I don't think I've properly thanked the writer yet."

"You can do it later today," Rothschild told him. "He's over there."

Chantel glanced over to the tall, rangy man who stood, chain-smoking nervously, on the edge of the set. She'd met him a handful of times in meetings and during preproduction. As she recalled, he had said little that hadn't dealt directly with his book or his characters. She sent him a vaguely friendly smile before turning back to the director.

As Rothschild outlined the scene, she pushed everything else out of her mind. All that would be left was the heartbreak and hope her character felt as her lover slipped away. Mechanically, their minds on angles and continuity, she and Sean went over their brief but poignant love scene.

"I think I should touch your face like this." Chantel reached up to rest her palm on his cheek and looked pleadingly into his eyes.

"Then I'll take your wrist." Sean wrapped his fingers around it, then turned her palm to his lips.

"I'll wait for you and so forth." Chantel skipped over the lines as one of the crew dropped a barn door into place with a clatter. She gave a small, broken sigh and pressed her cheek to his. "Then I'll start to bring my arms up."

"Let's try this." Sean took her shoulders, held her for a moment while they stared at each other, then placed two nibbling kisses on either side of her mouth.

"Oh, Brad, please don't go . . . Then I kiss you until your teeth rattle."

Sean grinned. "I'm looking forward to it."

"Let's run through it." Rothschild held up a hand. Women directors were still the exception to the rule. She couldn't afford to give herself, or anyone else, an inch. "I want a lot of steam when you get to the kiss," she told both of them. "Keep the tears coming, Chantel. Remember, deep in your heart you know he's not coming back."

"I really am a cad," Sean said pleasantly.

"Places." Extras scrambled to their marks. A few members of the camera crew broke off making plans for a poker game. "Quiet on the set." Rothschild moved over, too, until she had the best angle for Chantel's entrance. "Action."

Chantel dashed out on the platform, looking around frantically while groups of people milled around her. It all showed on her face, the desperation, the last flames of hope, the dream that wasn't ready to die. There would be a thunderstorm brewing, thanks to special effects. Lightning flashing, thunder rolling. Then she spotted Brad. She called out his name, pushing her way through the crowd until she was with him.

They rehearsed the scene three times before Rothschild was satisfied enough to roll film. Chantel's makeup and hair were freshened. When the clapper came down, she was ready.

Throughout the morning they perfected the first part of the scene, her search, the impatience and rush of the crowd, her meeting with Brad. Take after take she repeated the same moves, the same words, at times with the camera no more than a foot away.

On the sixth take, Rothschild finally gave

the signal for the rain. The sprinklers sent down a drizzle that misted over her as she stood facing Brad. Her eyes filled and her voice trembled as she begged him not to leave. Wet and cold, they continued to go over what would be five minutes on the screen until lunch break.

In her dressing room, Chantel stripped out of Hailey's clothes and handed them to the wardrobe mistress so that they could be dried. Her hair would be styled again, then soaked again, before she could call it a day.

The roses were gone, but she thought she could still smell them. When Larry came to the door to tell her that the reporter had arrived, she asked him to give her five minutes, then send him along.

She'd put it off too long, she told herself as she picked up the phone. It wasn't going to stop, and she'd reached the point where she could no longer ignore it.

"The Burns Agency."

"I need to speak to Matt."

"I'm sorry, Mr. Burns is in a meeting. May I —"

"This is Chantel O'Hurley. I have to speak to Matt now."

"Of course, Miss O'Hurley."

Chantel couldn't resist a slight smirk at how quickly the receptionist had changed her tune. Searching a drawer for the pack of cigarettes she kept for emergencies, she waited for Matt to come on the line.

"Chantel, what's up?"

"I need to see you. Tonight."

"Well, sweetheart, I'm kind of tied up. Why don't we make it tomorrow?"

"Tonight." Some of the panic fought its way through. Chantel lighted the cigarette and drew deeply. "It's important. I need help." She let the smoke out in a slow stream. "I really need your help, Matt."

Because he'd never heard fear in her voice before, he didn't question her. "I'll come by, what . . . eight?"

"Yes, yes, that's fine. I appreciate it."

"Can you tell me what it's about?"

"I can't. Not over the phone, not now." She was calming again, just knowing she was about to take a step seemed to help.

"Whatever you say. I'll be there tonight."

"Thanks." She hung up the phone just as the knock came at her door. Chantel carefully stubbed out her cigarette, tossed her still-damp hair back and ushered the reporter in with a gracious smile.

"Why in the hell didn't you tell me about this before?" Matt Burns paced around Chantel's spacious living room with an unfamiliar feeling of helplessness. In twelve years he'd scrambled his way up from mail clerk to assistant to top theatrical agent. He hadn't gotten there by not knowing what to do in any given situation. Now he had a hornet's nest on his hands, and he wasn't sure which way to toss it. "Damn it, Chantel, how long has this been going on?"

"The first phone call came about six weeks ago." Chantel sat on a low oyster-colored sofa and nursed a glass of mineral water. Like Matt, she didn't like the feeling of helplessness. She disliked having to ask someone else to do something about a problem of hers even more. "Look, Matt, the first couple of calls, the first couple of letters, seemed harmless." Ice clinked in her glass as she set it down, then picked it up again. "With my face plastered all over magazines and all over the screen, obviously I'll attract attention. Not all of it's healthy. I figured if I ignored it it would stop."

"But it didn't."

"No." She looked down at her glass, remembering the words printed on the card. *I'm watching you always. Always.* "No, it got worse." She shrugged, trying to pretend to herself, and to him, that it wasn't as bad as it sounded. "I had my number changed, and for a while it worked."

"You should have told me."

"You're my agent, not my mother."

"I'm your friend," he reminded her.

"I know." She held out a hand. Real friendships were few and far between in the world she'd chosen. "That's why I called you before I went off the deep end. I'm not a hysterical woman."

He laughed, then released her hand to pour himself another drink. "Anything but."

"When those roses — Well, I knew I had to do something, but I didn't know what."

"The *what* is to call the police."

"Absolutely not." She lifted a finger when he started to object. "Matt, I imagine you can write the scenario as easily as I can. We call the police, then the press gets hold of it. Headline: Chantel O'Hurley Haunted by Twisted Admirer. Whispered Phone Calls. Desperate Love Letters." She pulled a hand through her hair. "We might be able to laugh that off, even use it to a point, but it wouldn't be long before a few more unbalanced personalities decided to write me some fan letters. Or camp out at the front gate. I don't think I can handle more than one at a time."

"What if he's violent?"

"Don't you think I've thought of that?"

She plucked one of his French cigarettes from his pocket and waited for him to light it.

"You need protection."

"Maybe I do." She took a quick, hurried drag. "Maybe I'm just about ready to admit that, but I'm in the middle of a film. You bring cops on the set and people wouldn't stop talking."

"Since when has gossip worried you?"

"Never." She managed an easy smile. "Except when it's about something really personal. My, ah . . . extraordinary love affairs and hedonistic life-style are one thing. My life, as it really is, is quite another. No police, Matt, at least not yet. I need another alternative."

He took the cigarette from her and inhaled thoughtfully. Chantel's first job on the screen had been negotiated by him. He'd seen her through everything from shampoo commercials to feature films, and it was rare, very rare, for her to ask for help with something personal. In all the years he had known her, even Matt had seldom gotten beneath the image of the woman they had both manufactured.

"I think I have one. Trust me?"

"Haven't I always?"

"Sit tight. I'm going to make a call."

35

Chantel settled back and closed her eyes when Matt left the room. Maybe she was overreacting. Maybe she was being foolishly jumpy about a fan who'd taken admiration just a few steps too far.

I'm watching you . . . watching you. . . .

No. Unable to sit, Chantel sprang up to pace around the room. She enjoyed being watched — on the screen. She could accept being photographed whenever she swept in or out of a club, whenever she attended a party or a premiere. But this was . . . frightening, she admitted. As if someone were just outside the windows, looking in. The thought made her glance nervously over her shoulder. Of course there was no one there. She had the electronic gate, the walls, the security. But she couldn't stay locked in her house twenty-four hours a day.

She stopped by the antique mirror above the white marble fireplace. There was the face she was familiar with, the face critics had called devastating, incomparable, even heartlessly beautiful. A lucky accident, she sometimes thought, the combination of pearly skin, Nordic blue eyes and ice-sharp cheekbones. She'd done nothing to earn the face, the classic oval shape of it, the full, lush mouth or the thick mane of angel-blond hair. She'd been born with that, but she'd worked for the rest. And worked hard.

She'd been performing since she could walk, traveling endlessly around the country with her family in clubs and regional theater. She'd paid her dues long before she had come to Hollywood at nineteen, not starry-eyed but determined. In the years that had passed, she had won roles and lost them, had hawked shampoo and sold gallons of perfume in unapologetically sexy, often silly commercials. When her first break had come she'd been ready, more than ready, to play the soulless man-eater who stayed on screen less than twenty minutes. She'd stolen that movie from a pair of veterans and had gone on to star in one of her own. There'd been no looking back.

That first break had brought her the stardom she had always craved. And had, indirectly, nearly destroyed her life.

Yet, she'd survived, Chantel reminded herself as she faced her own reflection. She hadn't allowed what had happened all those years ago to ruin her. She refused to allow what was happening now to ruin her, either.

"He's coming right over."

She turned away from the mirror as Matt strode into the room again. "What?"

"I said he's coming right over. Let me fix you a real drink."

"No, I have to be on the set at six-thirty. Who's coming right over?"

"Quinn Doran. He might just be the answer, and since we go back a ways, I was able to . . . persuade him to think about it."

Chantel stuck her hands in the pockets of her white satin loungers. "Who is Quinn Doran?"

"He's sort of a private investigator."

"Sort of?"

"He runs a security business . . . corporate, small business, whatever. At one time he worked in some sort of covert operation. Might have been for our government, but I couldn't swear to it."

"Sounds fascinating, but I don't think I want a spy, Matt. A three-hundred-pound wrestler might be more appealing."

"And obvious," he reminded her. "You could hire yourself a couple of bruisers for bodyguards, sweetheart, but what you want here is brains — and discretion. That's Quinn." He finished off his drink and contemplated having another. "He doesn't do much of the legwork himself now. He has plenty of operatives or whatever they're called to handle that. Keeps himself available as a troubleshooter. But in this case I want you to have the best."

"And that's Quinn," Chantel mimicked,

dropping onto the arm of the sofa. "What's he supposed to do?"

"I don't have any idea. That's why I called him. He's a moody bastard," he said reminiscently. "Not too, well . . . polished, but I'd trust him with my life."

"Or, in this case, mine."

Matt's expression changed immediately. "Chantel, if you're really that worried —"

"No, no." With a wave of her hand, she brushed off his concern. "I have the feeling that this Quinn Doran of yours is likely to listen to what I have to say, roll his eyes and give me a lecture on how to handle the obscene phone caller. I don't like him already."

"You're just nervous." Matt patted her knee as he crossed to the bar. "You're allowed to be nervous, Chantel."

"No, I'm not." She smiled, determined to lighten her own mood. "Nerves don't fit the image. It's an image you helped me mold."

"You didn't need any help with that." With a smile for her, he turned back and studied the flow of white satin that suited her so well. "You were born with the talent. I just helped you expand it."

She tilted her head and gave him a long, luxurious smile. "How'd we do?"

"I'll say this, no one looking at you today

would think that you'd once mended your panty hose."

She laughed and slid down on the sofa. "You're so good for me, Matt."

"I've been telling you that for years. There's the bell. I'll get it."

Chantel picked up her warming mineral water and swirled it. If Matt thought Quinn Doran was an answer, she'd have to take his word for it. But it galled her, it galled her right down to the ground, to tell her personal problems to a stranger.

Then the stranger walked in.

If she had had to cast someone in the role of a spy, a private investigator or an alley fighter, her choice would have been Quinn Doran. He filled the archway to her living room, inches taller than Matt, inches broader in the shoulders, yet with a wiry leanness that made her think he could move fast and move well. The quick flutter of feminine approval she accepted as natural even before she looked at his face. Then she thought it unnatural.

He wasn't leading-man handsome, but he had tough go-to-hell looks that would make any woman's pulse uneven. Dark, thick hair curled over his ears and trailed over the collar of a denim work shirt. His skin was tanned and taut over strong facial bones, and the pale shade of his eyes seemed almost startlingly cool. His lashes were too long, too thick for a man, but they were anything but feminine. There was nothing about him that wasn't totally masculine. When he walked, he walked with the soft, measured stride of a man who knew how to stalk. His mouth turned up slightly as he crossed to her, but Chantel didn't see humor or appreciation in his eyes. She saw, recognized and stiffened against derision.

"So this is the ice palace," he said in a surprisingly beautiful voice. "And the queen."

Chapter Two

He'd seen her before, of course. On the screen she looked larger than life, indomitable, untouchable. The face, almost mystically perfect, could rule a man's fantasies. A facade. Quinn understood facades, how they could be formed, altered or hacked away as circumstances demanded. He wondered, as with a casual glance he took in everything about her, how much substance there was beneath that silk-and-satin exterior.

Matt had known Quinn too long to be disturbed by his cavalier attitude. "Chantel, Quinn Doran."

Satin slid over satin as she crossed her legs. With a lazy kind of grace, she offered her hand. "Charming," she murmured, stiffening as his fingers curled firmly over hers. He didn't shake her hand, nor did he bring it to his lips in the casual-European gesture she suddenly felt he was capable of. He just held it while his pale green eyes held hers. Her skin was like the satin she wore, smooth, fragrant and coolly feminine. His was hard, unyielding and darkened by the sun. They froze for a moment, her on the sofa, him on his feet, with their hands still locked. Chantel had been in combat with men before, and only once had she lost. She understood that the glove had been tossed down, and she accepted the challenge.

"Is it still vodka rocks?" Matt asked Quinn as he turned to the bar.

"Yeah." With a slight inclination of his head, Quinn indicated that he knew the game was on. He relaxed his fingers slowly to let her hand slide from his. "Matt tells me you have a problem."

"Apparently I do." Chantel plucked a cigarette from a porcelain holder on the table, then lifted a brow. When Quinn drew a lighter out of his pocket and flicked it on, she smiled and leaned a bit closer. "I'm afraid I don't know if you're the man to deal with it —" her gaze lifted and held his before she leaned back again "— Mr. Doran."

"I'm inclined to agree with you . . . Miss O'Hurley." For the second time their gazes locked, and something not entirely pleasant hummed between them. "But since I'm here, why don't you tell me about it?" Quinn accepted the glass from Matt, then shot him a look before he could speak.

"Why don't we let Miss O'Hurley fill me in, since it's her problem?"

As an agent, Matt knew when to negotiate and when to back off. "Fine, I'll just fill my mouth with a few of these canapés." He sat, leaving them to each other.

"I've been getting some annoying phone calls." She said it casually, but the tension showed briefly in the way her fingers curled and uncurled. Quinn was used to picking up on small details. At the moment he noticed that her hands were quite small and narrow, with long fingers, the rounded tips painted with clear lacquer. The fingers themselves were never quite still.

"Phone calls?"

"And letters." She moved her shoulders and the satin whispered quietly. "It started about six weeks ago."

"Obscene phone calls?"

Chantel lifted her chin, unable to resist the urge to look down her small, straight nose. "I suppose that would depend on your definition of obscene. Yours might be quite different than mine."

Humor touched his eyes and made them strangely appealing. She wondered fleetingly how many women had stepped into his lion's den and been devoured. "I'm sure it is. Go on."

"At first — at first you could say I was almost amused. It seemed harmless enough, though annoying. Then . . ." She moistened her lips and brought the cigarette to them. "Then he became a bit bolder, more explicit. It made me uneasy."

"You should change your number."

"I've done that. The phone calls stopped for about a week. They started again today."

As he leaned back, Quinn sampled the vodka. Like her, it was a quality brand. "You recognize the voice?"

"No, he whispers."

"You could change your number again." The ice clinked in his glass as he shrugged. "Or have the police put a tap on it."

"I'm tired of changing my number." With quick impatience, she stubbed out the cigarette. "And I don't want the police. I prefer to keep this discreet. Matt seems to think you're the answer to that."

Quinn drank again. The room was done in different shades of white, but it wasn't virginal. The very absence of color, with her at the center, was outrageously alluring. He was sure she knew it. In every one of her films she had acted the role of a woman who deliberately played on a man's needs, his weaknesses, his most private dreams. Quinn could drum up little sympathy for a woman who deliberately projected an image designed to arouse men, then complained about a few harmless phone calls.

"Miss O'Hurley, you're probably aware that men who make these kind of calls don't do anything but talk. I'd suggest you change your number again, then have one of your servants answer the phone for a while, until he gets tired of it."

"Quinn." Matt swirled his own drink. He had a habit of keeping in motion when under pressure, his hands, his feet. Now, he cleared his throat and tried to settle. "That's not much help."

"She can hire a bodyguard if it makes her feel better. Her security here could certainly be tightened."

"Maybe I need barbed wire, vicious guard dogs," Chantel interjected, and rose.

"That's the price you pay," Quinn told her coolly, "for being what you are."

"What I am?" Her eyes, already a vivid, searing blue, sharpened. "Oh, I see. I parade myself on the screen, I don't dress in burlap and wear a veil over my face, therefore I asked for what I got. And I deserve it."

Her cool beauty was compelling, but her passionate outburst was like seeing fire in ice. Quinn ignored the tightening in his gut and shrugged. "That's close enough."

"Thank you for your time," she said, and turned away. Before she could stop herself, she was whirling back. "Why don't you take a walk into the twentieth century? Just because a woman is attractive and doesn't disguise the fact doesn't mean she deserves to be abused — verbally, physically or emotionally."

"I don't believe I said an attractive woman, or any woman, deserves abuse," Quinn commented.

His careless tone only stoked the fires. "Just because I'm an actress and sexuality is part of my craft doesn't mean I'm fair game for any man who wants a piece of me. If I play the part of a murderer, it doesn't mean I should go on trial."

"You appeal to a man's most primitive fantasies, Miss O'Hurley, and you do it in Technicolor. There's bound to be a little backwash."

"So I should just take my medicine," she murmured. "You're an idiot. You're the kind of man who wears his brain below his belt. The kind who thinks if a woman agrees to have dinner with him she should pay for it with a romp between the sheets. Well, I can pay for my own dinner, Mr. Doran, and I can handle my own problems.

I'm sure you can find the door."

"Chantel," Matt began, but she turned on him like a cat. "I'll just have a few more canapés," he muttered.

"Miss O'Hurley."

"What?" Chantel spun around to face her tall, aging majordomo, then drew in a long, cleansing breath. "Yes, Marsh, what is it?"

It was the tone that had Quinn narrowing his eyes. There was an underlying straightforward quality to it that ignored any domestic caste system and spoke human to human. Though nerves had her body strung tight, she smiled at the old man.

"These were just delivered for you."

"Thank you." Chantel crossed the room to him and took the vase of daylilies. "I won't need you any more tonight, Marsh."

"Very good, Miss."

Stepping behind Quinn, she went to a table by the windows. "Why don't you show your friend out, Matt? I don't think —"

She had the card in her hands and was staring at it. Her fingers trembled momentarily before she crushed the paper. Before she could drop it on the floor, Quinn had her wrist and was slowly drawing the mangled note from her. What he read made his stomach tighten, this time in disgust.

"No more than I deserve?" Chantel's

voice was cold, almost detached, but her eyes, when Quinn looked into them, were terrified. He slipped the paper into his pocket as he took her arm.

"Why don't you sit down?"

"Was it another one?" Matt started toward them, but Quinn motioned to the bar.

"Get her a brandy."

"I don't want a drink. I don't want to sit down. I want you to go." When she started to pull her arm away, Quinn merely tightened his hold and led her to the sofa. "How often do you get one of these?"

"Nearly every day." She picked up a cigarette, then put it back.

"All of them as . . . direct?"

"No." She took the brandy and sipped at it, hating to admit she needed it. "That started a couple of weeks ago."

"What did you do with the notes?"

"I tossed out the first few. Then, when the tone started to change, I was going to burn them." The brandy warmed her but did nothing to settle her. "I kept them. I'm not sure why. I suppose I thought I should have them if things got out of hand."

"Call your servant back in. I want to ask him some questions. And go get the other letters."

His orders did what the brandy hadn't. Chantel felt her spine straighten. "It's none of your concern, Mr. Doran. We've already settled that."

"This just unsettled it." He drew the paper out of his pocket and watched her slight but definite recoil.

"I don't want your help."

"I didn't say I'd give it yet." He let that hang as they continued to stare at each other. "The letters? Unless you've got a better idea what to do about all this."

At that moment, at that one shimmering moment, she despised him. She could have hidden it. She was skilled enough. She didn't bother. Before she could speak, Matt laid a hand on her shoulder. His fingers moved as restlessly as hers.

"Please, Chantel. Think before you say anything."

She kept her eyes on Quinn's. "I wouldn't want to say what I'm thinking." When his lips curved again, she gritted her teeth. "Or perhaps I would."

"Chantel." Matt gave her shoulder a light squeeze. "I don't like ultimatums, but if we can't deal with Quinn, I'm going to call the police. No," he continued when her head shot back, "I mean it. You're a smart woman. Be practical."

She hated being backed into a corner. Quinn could see it. She was a woman who insisted on having the choice and the control in her own hands. It was something he could admire, even respect. Maybe, just maybe, there was more to Chantel O'Hurley than met the eye.

"All right, we'll do it your way. For now." She rose, at once regal and strong. "Don't badger Marsh." She met Quinn's eyes levelly. "He's old and getting frail. I don't want him upset."

"I haven't kicked a dog all day," Quinn told her.

"Only small children and kittens," she murmured, then swept from the room.

"Quite a woman, your client."

"She's all of that," Matt agreed. "And she's scared right down to her toes. She doesn't scare easily."

"I bet she doesn't." Quinn took out a cigarette and tapped it idly against the pack. He was forced to admit that he had thought she was simply dramatizing. The few sentences printed on the card had changed his mind. They were just short of vile. For Quinn, the line of demarcation between right and wrong was flexible, but the card fell well on the wrong side. Still, before he decided just how much he wanted to be involved, there were a few things he had to know.

He glanced back at Matt, watching him pace. "Just how close are the two of you?"

"We have a solid, mutually advantageous arrangement." Matt gave Quinn a sober smile. "And she doesn't sleep with me."

"You're slipping."

"She knows what she wants, and what she doesn't want. She wanted an agent. But I do care about her." He cast a worried look at the doorway. "She's already gone through enough."

"Enough of what?"

With a shake of his head, Matt sat again. "Another story, and nothing to do with this. Are you going to be able to help her?"

Quinn drew slowly on his cigarette. "I don't know."

"Excuse me." Marsh stood in the doorway, still dressed in his black suit and starched collar. "Miss O'Hurley said you wanted to speak with me."

"I wondered if you could tell me about the person who delivered the flowers." Quinn gestured toward them and watched the old man squint. Nearsighted, he thought.

"They were delivered by a young man, eighteen, perhaps twenty. He rang from the gate and explained that he had a delivery for Miss O'Hurley."

"Was he wearing a uniform?"

Marsh's brows knit as he concentrated. "I don't believe so. I can't say for certain."

"Did you happen to see his car?"

"No, sir. I took the flowers at the back door."

"Would you recognize him if you saw him again?"

"Perhaps. I think I might."

"Thank you, Marsh."

Marsh hesitated. Then, remembering his position, he bowed stiffly. "Very good, sir."

As he walked back into the hallway, Quinn heard Chantel stop him for a brief, murmured conversation. Her voice, he noticed, was soothing from a distance, quiet and easy. Up close, its smoky quality could twine around a man's nerve endings and make him want. She came back in, carrying a small pack of letters.

"I'm sure you'll find it fascinating reading," she said as she tossed them into Quinn's lap. "My guess is it's close to the technique you use to court women."

She'd regained her spirit, Quinn decided as he ignored her and opened the first envelope. The address on it, like the text inside, was printed in small block letters. The paper was dime-store quality. He could work for weeks and never trace it.

The first few notes he read were fawning in their admiration and subtly suggestive. And well written, Quinn added silently. The work of an educated person. As he went on, the prose and syntax remained good but the content deteriorated. Even a man who had seen and done what he had felt instant distaste. The writer went into graphic and pitiless detail, outlining his fantasies, his needs and his intentions. The last few letters added veiled hints that the writer was close by. Watching. Waiting.

When he'd finished, Quinn stacked the letters in a neat pile. "You sure you don't want the cops in on this?"

Chantel had seated herself across from him, and now she folded her hands in her lap. She didn't like him, she told herself. She didn't like the way he looked, the way he moved. She didn't like the fact that his voice was almost poetic, so very different from his lived in face. So why, if all this was true, did she feel as though she wanted, even needed, his help. She kept her eyes on his. Sometimes you made bargains with the devil.

"No, I don't want the police. I don't want publicity on this. What I want is for this man to be found and stopped."

Quinn rose and poured himself another drink. Both the glasses and ice bucket were Rosenthal. He appreciated elegant things, just as he appreciated the cruder things in life. Beer from a bottle or wine from a crystal glass, it hardly mattered, as long as your thirst was quenched. He appreciated beauty, but he wasn't duped by it. An outer shell meant nothing. He'd shed plenty of his own when the occasion had called for it.

Chantel O'Hurley had beauty, had elegance. If he took the job, by the very nature of it he was bound to discover how much was shell, how much was substance. That was what had him hesitating. He understood just how dangerous knowledge of another person could be — to all involved.

He could control the attraction he felt for her looks, as long as he chose to. His mood on that could change from day to day. What he wouldn't control, had never been able to control, was his curiosity as to what lay beneath the skin.

Swallowing his vodka, he turned back around. She was sitting back in her chair, and one would have thought from looking at her that she was relaxed, even aloof. The fingers on her left hand moved, just a little, curling together, spreading apart, as if she had managed to center her nerves only there. He shrugged and matched his mood to hers.

"Five hundred a day, plus expenses."

She lifted a brow. It was the only movement she made. With it, she conveyed a range of feeling — amusement, consideration and dislike. What it didn't show was the surge of relief that passed through her.

"That's a princely sum, Mr. Doran."

"You'll get your money's worth."

"That's something I insist on." Leaning back, she steepled her fingers under her chin. Her wrists were slender, and her hands were as delicate as her face. A diamond flashed on her right hand, then became as white and cool as the rest of her. "Just what do I get for five hundred a day plus expenses?"

His lips curved just before he brought the glass to them. "You get me, Miss O'Hurley."

She smiled a little. Sparring helped. She was back in control again, and the fear was ebbing. "Interesting." The look she sent him was designed to pin a man to the wall and make him beg. Quinn felt the punch and acknowledged the power. "What do I do with you?"

"You've got it backward." He walked to

her then, stopping by her chair to lean close. She caught a hint of scent, not cologne, not soap or powder, but raw and completely comfortable masculinity. Though she didn't retreat from it, she braced herself, recognizing her own attraction.

"Just what do I have backward, Mr. Doran?"

She looked like a painting, one he thought he'd seen in the Louvre a lifetime ago. "It's what I do with you. Five hundred a day, angel, and your trust. That's my price. You pay it and you get twenty-four-hour protection, starting with one of my men posted as a guard at that gate of yours."

"If I already have the gate, why do I need a guard?"

"Did it ever occur to you that a gate doesn't do a hell of a lot of good if you're going to open it up to anyone who asks?"

"What didn't occur to me was that I'd have to lock myself in."

"Get used to it, because whoever's sending you flowers doesn't have a clean bill of health."

Panic came and went in her eyes. He gave her points for how quickly she mastered it. "I'm aware of that."

"I need your schedule. Starting to-morrow, one of my men goes with you every time you stick your pretty nose out the door."

"No." The O'Hurley stubbornness came through as she rose to face him. "For five hundred a day I want you, Doran. You're the one Matt trusts, and you're the one I'm paying for."

They stood close, very close. He could smell the scent that seemed to seep through her pores, neither quiet nor subtle. The perfection of her face could take a man's breath away. Her hair swept back from it in a glorious cascade, like an angel's. If a man touched it, would he find heaven or be cast from the clouds? When it came to that, Quinn wouldn't worry about the consequences.

"You might regret it," he murmured, then smiled slowly.

So she might. Chantel already knew that, but pride wouldn't let her back down. "I pay for you, Mr. Doran. That's the deal."

"You're the boss." He lifted his drink to her. "Two of my men will come by in the morning to wire the phone."

"I don't want —"

"I don't take the job if you tie my hands." His easy smile was gone as quickly as it had formed. "We tap the phone, maybe he says something to give himself away, maybe we get lucky and trace it. Just think of us as doctors." He smiled at her again, enjoying himself. "If you want to say something intimate to one of your . . . friends, don't worry. We've heard it all and more."

Temper had always been the most difficult of her emotions to master. It surged up and was fought back down before she spoke again. "I'm quite sure you have. What else?"

"I'll take the letters with me. It's doubtful we'll be able to trace the paper, but we'll give it a shot. Now is there anyone you know who you think could be doing this?"

"No." The answer came immediately and with complete confidence. He decided to run a check on everyone close to her.

"Dump anyone in the last few months that may be carrying a torch for you?"

"Thousands."

"Cute." He drew a pad and the stub of a pencil out of his pocket. "I need the names of who you've slept with. We'll go back three months."

"Go to hell," she said sweetly, then started to sit. He caught her by the wrist.

"Look, I'm not going to play games with you. I'm not personally interested in how many men you've had in your bed. This is business."

"That's right." She tossed her head back. "My business."

Her skin was warmer than it looked. That was something he filed away to think about later. "One of them might just have gone off the deep end. Maybe you slept with him a couple times and it gave him delusions of grandeur. Think about it. This all started six weeks ago, so who were you with before that?"

"No one."

Annoyance covered his face as he tightened his hold. "Give me a break, angel. I haven't got all night."

"I said no one." She yanked her arm away. For a moment she wished she could rattle off a dozen names, two dozen names, just to see him sweat. "Believe whatever you like."

"I tell you what I don't believe, and that's that you spend your evenings alone, darning socks."

"I don't jump into bed with every man who passes within five feet of me." In a calculated move, she dropped her gaze down as if measuring the distance between them.

"It looks like about ten inches to me," he murmured.

"Sorry to disappoint you, but I have to be interested first, and I haven't been. Besides,

I've been working, and it tends to take up a great deal of my time." Unconsciously she rubbed at her wrist, where his fingers had pressed. "Satisfied?"

"Come on, Quinn, ease off." Feeling trapped in the middle, Matt moved over and put an arm around Chantel's shoulders. "She's had it rough enough."

"It's not my job to hold her hand." Quinn scooped up the letters, annoyed by the twinge of self-disgust he felt. "I'll be back tomorrow. What time do you get up?"

"Five-fifteen." She couldn't resist a smirk when he only stared at her. "I leave for the studio at five forty-five. That's a.m., Mr. Doran. Can you handle it?"

"You just write the check. Fifteen hundred in advance."

"You'll have it. Good night, Mr. Doran. It's been unusual."

"Do yourself a favor and don't answer your phone any more tonight." With that, he nodded to Matt and strode out. Chantel waited for the sound of the door closing behind him. She went to the coffee table and drew out another cigarette.

"Your friend's a bastard, Matt."

"Always has been," he agreed. "But he's the best."

Chapter Three

Chantel had thought she wouldn't sleep. The house had seemed so enormous around her, and so enormously quiet. But she had climbed into bed with a vision of Quinn Doran hovering in her mind. Just the thought of him made her furious, insulted her intelligence, nipped at her ego. And made her feel safe.

She slept only six hours, but she slept deeply.

Music woke her, pouring from the wall unit beside the bed. She rolled over, surrounded by pillows, covered with ivory linen sheets and nothing else.

The bed had been one of the first luxuries she had indulged herself with, almost before she could afford it. It was huge and old, with a carved cherrywood headboard that had made her think of princesses waking up from a hundred years of sleep. Growing up, she had invariably slept in hotel beds, and she'd decided that a sinfully beautiful bed was something she deserved to indulge herself in when she signed her first film contract. A small part in a full-length feature had been enough to pin her hopes on. Years later, when she awoke in the antique four-poster it still gave her the same satisfaction.

She thought back to the time when she had still lived in the small apartment in L.A. The bed had taken up the entire room, and she had had to crawl over it to reach the doorway. Her two sisters had visited once, and the three of them had stretched across it and talked and giggled for hours.

She wished they could be with her now. The feeling of safety would be more tangible.

She'd nearly told Maddy about the letters and calls when she'd gone to New York a few weeks before. Part of her had wanted to, needed to, but Maddy had been so preoccupied. She'd been entitled, Chantel reminded herself as she sat up and stretched. Her play had been nearly ready to open, and her heart had been wrapped up in the man who was backing it. All for a good cause, Chantel thought with a smile. The play was a smash, and Maddy was planning her wedding.

He'd better be good to her, Chantel thought as the old protective instinct rose up in her. She had had to watch one sister go through a miserable marriage. She couldn't bear it if Maddy was hurt, as well.

Maddy would be fine, she reassured herself. Just as Abby was fine. They had both found the right man at the right time. So she had one sister planning a wedding and the other preparing for the birth of her third child. She couldn't spoil all that by dumping her problems on them now. Besides, she was the eldest triplet, if only by a matter of minutes. To Chantel, that meant that she had the responsibility to be the strongest. They would be there for her, of course, just as she would be there for them. But she was the oldest.

They'd come so far. Chantel sat in the middle of the lush bed and looked around a room that was larger than the whole of her first apartment in California. Why was it she felt as though she still had so far to go?

Now wasn't the time for philosophizing. After turning up the volume on the radio, she climbed out of bed and prepared to face another day on the set.

Quinn wasn't accustomed to rising before dawn. It was much more his style to see the night through and find his bed at sunrise rather than climbing out of it at that hour. Not that he didn't appreciate an L.A. sunrise. It was simply more to his taste to watch the sky take on color after a night of celebration — in bed or out.

He drove across town under a pink and mauve sky, casting an occasional look of mild contempt at a jogger. Designer sweat suits weren't his style. If he wanted to tone up, he went to the gym. And not one of those pastel-walled spas where they piped in classical music, a real gym. You didn't see cute leotards there, and the sweat ran as free and healthy as the four-letter words. A man's world — and no one drank carrot juice frappé. A woman like Chantel O'Hurley wouldn't poke her million-dollar nose through the front door.

Quinn shifted in his seat and scowled at nothing in particular. He couldn't remember the last time a woman had made him uncomfortable. Chantel's looks were designed to make a man squirm — and ache. The hell of it was she knew it and, Quinn was certain, enjoyed it.

He couldn't let that be a problem. She was paying him to do a job. The only thing he could be concerned about from this point on was her security. The check she would give him entitled her to the best, and he *was* the best. Besides, he didn't care for the content of the letters she'd shown him.

65

Not that Quinn was a supporter of the women's movement. To his way of thinking, men and women were different. End of story. If a woman walking by a construction site was insulted because she got a few whistles or invitations, he figured she should walk someplace else. After all, that was just good clean fun. There'd been nothing clean, or fun, in the letters, though. And Chantel hadn't looked insulted, either. If he knew anything, Quinn knew what genuine fear looked like.

Sooner or later he would find out who had written them. That would take patience. In the meantime, he'd give Chantel the round-the-clock protection she was paying for. Remembering her face, Quinn acknowledged that that would take willpower. He had it, he thought with a shrug as he pulled up to the iron gates. Besides, chances were that she'd look like a hag at this hour of the morning.

He reached out the window and leaned on the buzzer.

"Yes?"

The frown moved into his eyes. Even in one word, Chantel's voice was easily recognizable. He hadn't expected her to answer the intercom herself. "Doran," he said curtly.

"You're prompt."

"You get what you pay for."

There was no answer, but the gates slowly swung open. Quinn cruised through them, then stopped to make certain they shut behind him.

In the daylight, he got a better look at the lay of the land. Anyone determined enough could find his way over the wall. He and a partner had once scaled a sheer cliff in Afghanistan with nothing more than rope and nerve.

The trees that flowered over the lawn sent up a sweet scent. And would provide more-than-adequate cover for an intruder. He was going to have to get a good look at the alarm system in the house, though he knew anything that could be put in could be deactivated.

Quinn pulled up just beyond the steps, then got out to lean on the hood of his car. You couldn't hear any traffic from here. Just the sound of birds. He took out a cigarette. A glance around showed him a few floodlights, maybe a dozen ground lights, obviously placed more for aesthetic purposes than for added security. After a look at his watch, Quinn decided to walk around the house and check a few things out for himself.

Perhaps out of spite, Chantel decided to

let Quinn cool his heels outside while she dallied in her dressing room. Under other circumstances she might have invited him in for a quick cup of coffee before the limo arrived. She wasn't feeling gracious. Instead, she took her time, bundling her hair back from her face, checking the contents of her bag, then writing a few instructions for her maid. When the buzzer from the gate rang again, she spoke to her driver, then gathered up her script. She turned toward the bedroom and walked into Quinn. He watched initial shock turn to anger.

"What the hell are you doing in here?"

"Just checked out your security system." He leaned against the doorway and noted, with a quick twinge, that regardless of the hour she looked fantastic. "It's pitiful. A Boy Scout with two merit badges could get past it."

Chantel settled the strap of her bag on her shoulder and promised herself she would pay Matt back if it was the last thing she ever did. "When it was installed I was assured it was the best on the market."

"Supermarket, maybe. I'll have my men beef it up."

She'd been born practical, and the years had done nothing to change that. "How much?"

"Don't know for sure until they're into it. Three to five, I'd say."

"Thousand?"

"Sure. Like I said, you —"

"Get what you pay for," she murmured, walking around him. "All right, Mr. Doran, you go right ahead." As she spoke, she moved to her nightstand. "But the next time you decide to check out the system, I wouldn't advise you sneaking into my bedroom." When she turned, she had a pearl-handled .22 in her hand. "I tend to be nervous."

Quinn regarded the gun with a raised brow. He'd been on the wrong end of one plenty of times before. "Know how to use one of those, angel?"

"You just pull this little trigger here." She smiled. "Of course, my aim's terrible. I'd point at your leg and end up shooting you right through the brain."

"There's only one rule about guns," he began, Quinn scowled over her shoulder. When Chantel turned to look, he was on her. With a move too quick to judge, he had the gun in his hand and her beneath him on the bed. "The rule is, don't point one unless you intend to use it."

She didn't squirm beneath him, but lay still, letting the heat of fury and dislike pour out. With a casual gesture he flipped open the pistol's chamber.

"It's not loaded."

"Of course it's not. I wouldn't keep a loaded gun in the house."

"A gun's not a souvenir." He closed it again before he looked down at her. Her face was untouched by makeup, and it was as beautiful as it was furious. Despite himself, Quinn found the combination very much to his liking. Her body was small and strong beneath his, not as cushioned and feminine as he'd expected. But her scent was there, as it had been the night before, outrageously feminine.

"Nice bed," he murmured, unable to resist the urge to sweep his gaze down to her mouth. He thought, but couldn't be sure, that her heartbeat increased.

"Your approval means everything to me, Mr. Doran. Now, if you don't mind, I have to get to work."

How many other men had pinned her between their bodies and this wide, firm mattress? How many other men had felt this wild, edgy flare of desire? Both thoughts ran through his head before he could stop them. Because they did, he rolled aside and yanked her to her feet. But she was still close.

"Maybe we'll keep this business," he told her quietly. "And maybe we won't."

Though her pulse was racing, Chantel wasn't dishonest enough to blame it on temper. Desire was something she understood, even if she had rarely felt it for a man. It was also something that could be controlled. Instinct warned her that it was vital to do that now, and to continue to do so, when it applied to Quinn.

"You tempt me to put bullets in that gun, Mr. Doran."

"It wouldn't hurt." Quinn dropped it back in her bedside drawer. "And make it Quinn, angel. After all, we've been to bed together." Taking her arm, he escorted her downstairs and outside.

"Good morning, Robert." Chantel smiled at her driver as he opened the back door of the limo. "Mr. Doran will be accompanying me to the studio for a few days."

"Very good, Miss O'Hurley."

Quinn didn't miss the wistful look the driver sent him before they were closed in behind smoked glass. "How does it feel to infatuate the male of the species?"

Chantel settled back. "He's just a boy."

"Does that make a difference?"

Behind her dark glasses, Chantel shut her

eyes. "Oh, I forgot. I'm one of those heart-less women who tease and flaunt, then toss men aside after I've drained them, like empty pop bottles."

Amused, Quinn stretched out long legs. "That pretty much covers it."

"You have a remarkable disdain for women, Mr. Doran."

"No, you're wrong. Women happen to be one of my favorite pastimes."

"Past—" Chantel caught herself before she sputtered. She drew her glasses com-pletely off, wishing she could see if he was baiting her or speaking the simple truth. Wanting to believe the worst of him, she went with the latter. "You're a classic chau-vinist, Mr. Doran. I'd thought your species nearly extinct."

"We're a hardy breed, angel." He pushed a button and watched the compact bar rotate toward him. Quinn considered mixing a Bloody Mary but settled for straight orange juice.

Replacing her glasses, Chantel decided against beating her head against a brick wall. "I prefer not to introduce you as my bodyguard. I can do without that sort of speculation."

"Fine. How do you want to handle it?"

"They'll just assume you're my lover."

Coolly she took the glass of juice from him and sipped. "I'm accustomed to that sort of speculation."

"I bet. It's your game. Play it any way you want."

She handed him back the glass. "I intend to. And what will you do?"

"My job." As they passed through the studio gates, he drained the glass. "You just smile pretty at the cameras, angel, and don't worry about it."

She found that her jaw was tensed so tightly it hurt. Acting on impulse, Chantel turned to him, and curled her fingers into his shirt. "Oh, Quinn, it's just that I'm so frightened. I'm so very frightened. Not knowing from one minute to the next if I'm safe." Her voice broke as she leaned closer. "I can't tell you what it means to me just to know you'll be there. Protecting me. I'm defenseless, vulnerable. And you're so . . . strong."

She was close, so close he could see her eyes flutter shut behind the tinted glasses. Her body trembled lightly as she leaned into him. Desire flared, along with a need to comfort and protect. She was soft, pliant and helpless. As he drew her nearer, her scent tangled around his senses until his head throbbed with it. "You don't have to

73

worry," he murmured. "I'm going to take care of you."

"Quinn." Her head tilted up until her lips were only a whisper away from his. When she felt him tense, she jerked back and pressed something into his hand. "Your check," she said carelessly, then stepped out of the limo.

Quinn sat for a full ten seconds and wondered why he'd never entertained thoughts of strangling a woman before. When he stepped out beside her, he curled his fingers around her arm. "You're good. Very, very good."

"Yes, I am." She gave him a slow, easy smile. "And I get much better."

As Chantel went through her morning routine of makeup and hairstyling, Quinn simply observed. There were a dozen people Chantel came in contact with during the first hour alone. There were other actors, technicians and a parade of assistants. He'd want a list, and he was beginning to realize just how extensive it would be. Whoever was hounding her obviously knew her routine. That made the people she worked with his priority.

"Miss — ah, Chantel." Larry stopped by her side with a cup of fresh coffee.

"Oh, thanks. You read my mind."

He preened a bit, pleased. "I knew the hair was going to take longer this morning." He watched as the stylist patiently threaded pearls through the already complicated arrangement. "You're going to be just beautiful for the ballroom scene."

"A far cry from yesterday." She sipped the coffee. "If they'd watered me one more time, I'd have melted."

"Miss Rothschild said the dailies were great. I checked."

"Thanks." She caught sight of Quinn's reflection in the mirror and decided that moment was as good a time as any. "Larry, this is Quinn Doran, a friend of mine." Only years of training kept her from choking on the word as she held a hand over her shoulder for Quinn's. "Larry's my right hand. And often my left, as well. Quinn's going to watch the filming for a few days."

"Oh, well . . ." Larry cleared his throat. "That's nice."

Quinn saw that the young man thought it was anything but. Another conquest, he thought. But he couldn't afford to feel sympathy, only suspicion.

"I'll keep out of the way," Quinn promised, making the most of it by rubbing his thumb over Chantel's knuckles. "I just want to see Chantel at work."

"Isn't that sweet?" Chantel said with a brilliant smile. "Quinn's between jobs at the moment and has time on his hands. Now don't be sensitive, darling." She gave his hand a pat before drawing hers away. "We all understand how difficult the job market is, especially for botanists." Satisfied, Chantel rose. "I have to get into costume."

"They've scheduled publicity shots this morning," Larry told her after an uncertain glance at Quinn. "As soon as you're ready, you're supposed to go to the ballroom set."

"Fine."

"I'll go with you, darling." Quinn slipped an arm around her shoulders and squeezed, just a few degrees too hard. "You might need some help with buttons and snaps."

"Ease up, Doran," she muttered as they walked away. "I'm wearing a strapless dress for this scene, and I can't afford the bruises."

"You tempt me to put them where they won't show. A botanist?"

"I've always been attracted to the sensitive, introspective type."

"Like Larry?"

"He's my assistant. Leave him alone."

"Don't tell me how to do my job."

"He's a nice boy, he came with excellent references and —"

"How long ago?"

Annoyed, Chantel yanked open the door of her trailer. "About three months."

When the door shut at his back, Quinn drew out a notebook. "Let's have his full name."

"Larry Washington. But I don't see —"

"You don't have to. What about the makeup guy?"

"George? Don't be absurd, he's old enough to be my grandfather."

Quinn merely shifted his gaze until it met hers. "The name, angel. There's no age limit on a disturbed mind."

She muttered it, then swept back into the private dressing alcove. "I don't like the way you work, Doran."

"I'll notify the complaint department." Lowering to the arm of a chair, he took a quick, interested look around her dressing room. Like her home, it was meticulously decorated in white on white. "While we're at it, give me the names of the rest of the men you deal with on the set."

There was a brief, pregnant pause. "All of them?"

"That's right."

"That's impossible," she told him. "I couldn't possibly remember everyone. Oh, most by sight and by first name, but not everything about everyone."

"Then find out."

"I have a job to do. I can't —"

"So do I. Get me the names."

Chantel yanked up the zipper at her back and scowled at the wall that separated them. "I'll see if Larry can get me a list."

"No, you won't. I don't want to rouse anyone's suspicions."

"All right, all right." For a moment she was convinced the cure was more trouble than the problem. Then she remembered the contents of the last note. Like it or not, she needed Quinn. "The assistant director's name is Amos Leery. The cinematographer's Chuck Powers. And damn it, they didn't walk into town yesterday. They've been in the business for years. They have families."

"What difference does that make? An obsession's an obsession." When she walked back into the room, Quinn was still sitting, scribbling in his notebook.

"What about the director?"

"The director's a woman." Chantel slipped off her watch and laid it aside. "I think we can rule her out."

"What about the —" He made the mistake of looking up as he spoke. The words stopped because his thought processes

78

simply disintegrated. She was wearing red, a hot, vibrant red that seemed to lick at her skin. The dress scooped low and snug at her breasts, then followed the lines of her body. The skirt hung straight, hitched up on one side nearly to the hip, where it was secured by a circlet of glittering stones. His mouth went suddenly and completely dry.

Chantel saw the look, recognized it. Normally it would have made her smile, either with pleasure or in automatic response. Now she found she couldn't, because her heart was thudding too hard. He rose slowly and she stepped back. It wouldn't occur to her until much later that it was the first time in her life she had retreated from a man.

"I'll have to give you the rest later," she said quickly. "They'll be waiting for me on set."

"What are you supposed to be in that?" He didn't take another step toward her. Self-preservation held him back.

Chantel moistened her lips. "A woman out for revenge."

He looked at her again, gradually, up, then down, then up again until their eyes met. "I'd say you get it."

Making a conscious effort, she drew in a breath, then let it out again. Play the role, she told herself. It was always possible to play the role. "Like it?" Deliberately she turned a slow circle, revealing the daring plunge at the back.

"It's a bit much for seven-thirty in the morning."

"Think so?" She smiled, more comfortable now. "Wait until you see the hardware that goes with it. Cartier's lending us a necklace and earrings. Two hundred and fifty thousand dollars worth of all that glitters. We'll have two armed guards and a very nervous jeweler here shortly."

"Why not use paste? It shines, too."

"Because the real thing makes for better publicity. Coming?"

He stopped her at the door with just a fingertip on her bare shoulder. Each of them felt the jolt. "One question. You wear anything under that?"

She managed another smile only because her hand was already on the knob. "This is Hollywood, Mr. Doran. We leave little details like that up to your imagination." She stepped out, hoping the constriction in her chest would ease before the first take.

By noon, Quinn had been forced to revise his opinion of Chantel at least in one area. She wasn't the pampered, temperamental prima donna he had expected. She worked like a horse — a thoroughbred, perhaps, but she went through her paces time and time again without complaint.

She'd been gracious to the photographers even when the session had run on for ninety minutes. She hadn't snapped at the makeup artist, as one of her co-stars had, when it had been time for yet another retouch. The temperature on the set was sizzling, thanks to the lights, but she didn't wilt. Between takes she sipped from an ever-present glass of mineral water, unable to sit, because wardrobe had fussed about creases in her costume.

Two armed guards kept their eyes trained on her, and on the quarter million in jewels she wore. They suited her, he was forced to admit — the thick gold band crusted with diamonds and rubies that circled her neck, the symphony of diamonds and hot red stones that dripped from her ears. She wore them with the ease of a woman who knew she deserved them.

Quinn stayed well off the set and wondered how the actors could take the sheer monotony of repetition.

"Incredible, isn't it?"

Quinn turned his head and glanced at the tall, graying man beside him. "What's that?"

"How it takes them hours and hours to film a two minute scene." He pulled out a thin black cigarette and lighted it from the butt of another. "I don't know why I come. It makes me nervous, but I can't stay away while they dissect my brainchild."

Quinn lifted a brow. "No, I suppose not."

He drew in smoke deeply before he smiled. "I'm not mad — or perhaps I am. I wrote the screenplay. Rather, I wrote what it appears this will loosely resemble." He offered a well-kept, rather thin hand. "James Brewster."

"Quinn Doran."

"Yes, I know. You're Miss O'Hurley's friend." He smiled again with a negligent shrug. "Word travels fast in small towns. She's quite brilliant, isn't she?"

"I don't know much about it."

"Oh, I assure you, she is. There was really no one else who could be Hailey. Cold, vindictive, clawing, and at the same time vulnerable and desperate for love. One of the few things I don't worry about as far as this little extravaganza goes is Chantel's interpretation of Hailey."

"She seems to know what she's doing."

"More, she feels what she's doing." Brewster took another quick puff as the crew set up for the next take. "It gives me enormous pleasure just to watch her."

Quinn slipped his hands into his pockets and mentally added Brewster to his growing list of men to check out. "She's an extraordinarily beautiful woman."

"That goes without saying. But then, to use a cliché, that's only skin deep. It's what's inside Chantel O'Hurley that fascinates."

Quinn's eyes narrowed fractionally. "And what's that?"

"I would say, Mr. Doran, that every man would have to discover that for himself."

The director called for quiet, and Brewster lapsed into a nervous silence. Quinn contemplated his own considerations.

She did seem to feel the part. The key scene called for her to confront her lover three years after he had left her, alone and abandoned. Even after a half a dozen takes, her eyes would frost over on cue, her voice would take on just the necessary hint of venom. On a dance floor crowded with people, she set out to seduce and humiliate. Chantel did both with such apparent ease that Quinn felt she must enjoy it.

Even to him, a man who'd learned how to look beyond illusions, it seemed that she was only aware of the man in whose arms she danced. There might not have been any cameras, any technicians, any dollies or lifts.

It went on for hours, but Quinn was patient. It interested him to see that whenever a break lasted longer than five minutes her assistant appeared at her elbow with a fresh glass of mineral water. More than once the assistant director came over to take her hand and murmur to her. The makeup artist retouched her face time and again, as though it were a rare canvas.

It was after seven before they wrapped. They had taken an hour for lunch, and apart from that, Quinn calculated, she had been on her feet for fourteen hours. All in all, he decided, he'd rather spend eight hours digging ditches.

"Ever think of another line of work?" Quinn asked her as they closed themselves in her trailer again.

"Oh, no." Chantel eased out of her shoes and felt her arches cramp instantly. "I love the glamour."

"Where was it?"

The smile came automatically. "You catch on fast. If she'd called for one more take, just one more, I was going to ask you to shoot her in the knee. Get the zipper for me, will you? My arms are like rubber."

"That's because you had them wrapped around Carter for most of the day."

"Just one of the perks of the job." She arched her back as Quinn brought the zipper down below her hips.

"He's okay, if you like the smooth poster-boy type."

She looked over her shoulder with a half smile. "I adore them."

"Ever think it might be Carter who's sending you flowers?"

She stiffened a bit, then walked into the dressing area. "He's too busy trying to untangle himself from his third wife. Besides, I've known him for years."

"People change, or do the unexpected. And you spend several hours a day in a clinch with him."

"That's work."

"Nice work if you can get it. In any case, you shouldn't trust anyone."

"Except you."

"That's right. Brewster seemed pretty taken with you, too."

"Brewster? The writer?" Really amused, Chantel walked back in, still buttoning her blouse. "James is much more interested in his characters than the people who play them. And he's been happily married for twenty-odd years. Don't you ever read the gossip-columns?"

"Never miss them." He stopped in the act of reaching for a cigarette when she sat abruptly and grabbed her foot. "Problem?"

"It's always after you take those damn things off that you're in agony." She winced, swore and kneaded. "I can tell you, it was a man who invented the high heel — the same one who invented the bra."

"It's you women who wear the things," he pointed out, but knelt down and took her foot in his hand. "Got you in the arch?"

"Yes, but —" Her protest died on her lips as he began to press. With a long, sincere sigh, she leaned back. "Yes, that's wonderful. You've missed your calling. You could make a fortune as a masseur."

"You should see what I could do for the rest of you."

She opened one eye. "We'll just stick with the feet, thanks. If I were a few inches taller, or Sean a few inches shorter, I could have gotten away with flats for most of the shots."

"I'll tell you this, his love scenes with you seemed pretty sincere."

"They're supposed to." Bone-tired, she opened both eyes. "Look, we're professionals. It looked that way because we played it that way, not because either one of us has any physical interest in the other."

"It looked like interest from my angle. Especially when he put his hand on your —"

"Try another tune, Doran."

"I think you're about to tell me how to do my job again."

"I'd like you to do your job," she shot back, "instead of harping on a man just because he's good at his work."

"Just checking him out, angel."

"I don't want my friends and associates spied on."

"If you want someone who's afraid to step on toes, you hired the wrong man."

"I've come to that conclusion several times myself." She couldn't have said why her temper was building so quickly, but his hands moving slowly up and down the arch of her foot were doing things they shouldn't to her system. She wanted him out and gone. "Why don't you take a walk, Doran?" She jerked her foot away. "You're just not my style." Rising, she stepped around him. "You can keep the change."

"Fine." He was as angry as she, and just as baffled as to the cause. He only knew that for one quick moment he'd felt something for her, something soft and easy. It was gone now, erased as if it had never been. In its place was the anger, and a need, just as strong, that demanded physical release. "I might as well take a bonus while I'm at it."

He grabbed her. She'd known he wouldn't be gentle. His hand tangled in her hair as his mouth came down on hers. She'd known he would show little finesse. What she hadn't known, or hadn't admitted, was that she could respond so completely.

No man held her when she didn't choose to be held. No man took from her what she didn't willingly offer. Yet he *was* holding her, and she found nothing within herself to make him stop. His face was rough against her, and his fingers dug into her skin as he held her close. Defending herself should have been simple, even automatic, yet she didn't struggle in his arms. Her knees trembled, but she didn't even feel it. Everything was bound up in the sensation of his mouth on hers and the explosion of the taste of him. Delectable. Her lips parted and invited him in.

He rarely worried about consequences, and even less frequently questioned his instincts. When he had felt the need to touch her, to take her this way, he had done so. He was already paying for it. She was more than he had imagined she could be. Softer, smoother, warmer. It wasn't an image he held in his arms but a passionate, hot-blooded woman. Even as he discovered and explored the flavor and texture of her lips, he understood that he needed more. That was the trap, and he'd fallen right into it.

He drew her away because he wanted to see her face after she had tasted him. Her eyes opened slowly, so dark, so very blue that for an instant he was more vulnerable to her than either of them could have guessed. He felt the need shift to an ache, and the ache to uncertainty, before he pulled himself back.

"It's been an interesting day, angel." And one he was afraid he wouldn't easily forget. "Why don't you tell Matt to find you some-body else?"

It had been a long time since she had felt rejection. It hurt more than she remembered. Training and pride had her straightening and kept her voice icy cool. "If you've finished your show of male dominance, you can go." The image was back, even before her pulse had started to level. "If I hear of someone who needs a bodyguard for their poodle, I'll give them your card."

Chantel turned away when the phone rang. She picked up the receiver, then looked over her shoulder until she saw Quinn open the door. With a toss of her head, she brought it back to her ear. "Yes, hello."

The voice was too familiar now, and a degree more frightening. "I've waited all day to talk to you. You're so beautiful, so exciting. All day I've been imagining how we would —"

"Why don't you stop?" Control snapped as she shouted into the phone. "Why don't you just leave me alone?" Before she could slam the receiver down, Quinn snatched it out of her hand.

"Don't be angry." The edgy desperation in the voice had him tensing. "I love you. I can make you happy, happier than you've ever been."

"Miss O'Hurley's happier without you," Quinn said calmly. "You really should stop bothering her."

There was a long silence, and Quinn heard the breathing on the other end of the phone grow heavier. "She doesn't need you. She needs me. She needs me," the voice repeated before the connection was broken. Quietly Quinn replaced the receiver. Chantel's back was to him, but after a moment she turned around.

He could see that she'd worked hard, even in those few moments, to regain her composure. But her skin was as white as the room around them. "I thought you'd gone."

"So did I." He made it a policy never to

apologize for his actions. It was not that he didn't believe he could be wrong, just that apologies tended to weaken his position. In this case, he decided to come as close as possible without crossing the line. "Look, we don't have to like each other much to get this job done, and I don't like to leave things before they're finished. Why don't we just forget about what happened before."

She didn't care for compromises any more than Quinn did for apologies. But she cared less for the thought of going on alone. To satisfy both her needs and her pride, she gave him a bland smile. "Did something happen before?"

He acknowledged the gibe with a slight nod. "Not a thing. Let's get out of here."

Chapter Four

Chantel had long ago acknowledged that one couldn't have both privacy and fame. In order to achieve and maintain the second, the first almost invariably had to be sacrificed. If she went out for a quiet dinner with a friend, she would read about it the next day. If she danced with another celebrity, there would be pictures and speculation before the music stopped. According to the press, her life was full of men, full of wild, sizzling romance and blistering affairs. She accepted that. She was also shrewd enough to know that if she were rude or belligerent to the paparazzi both her reputation and her photographs would be unflattering. So she was willing, within reason, to court them and present a glamorous and unflappable image to the public.

But the tap on her phone and the guard at her gate were entirely different. They weren't part of the creamy silk-and-diamonds mystique she'd chosen to develop. If she had the choice . . . Every time that thought ran through her head, Chantel gritted her teeth and reminded herself that she didn't.

She should be grateful. It was difficult to acknowledge that fact, but she knew she should be. Since the phone call in her dressing room there had been nothing — no letters, no flowers, no whispering voice. She told herself she should be relieved. Instead, she felt as though she were waiting for the other shoe to drop.

During the week her work kept her too busy to think. She could, for a few hours a day, plunge herself into Hailey's character and her problems. As long as the film was rolling and the pressure was on, it was difficult to think of her own personal crises. Work had gotten her through other rough periods. She counted on its doing the same for her now.

But it was Saturday and the film was going smoothly, so she had no call. Normally she treasured mornings when she could lounge in bed for a few extra hours, indulging in the things that were reported to be part of her everyday life.

By seven she was awake. Disgusted, she ordered herself back to sleep. At seven-fifteen she was staring at the ceiling and thinking a great deal too much for her own peace of mind. Beautiful, glamorous women were supposed to sleep until noon, then pamper themselves with massages and facials. She'd have believed that herself if she hadn't been in the game so long.

Tossing the covers aside, she went into the office that adjoined her dressing room. Of all the rooms in her home, this one, and only this one, showed the other side of her. The furnishings, though sophisticated, were simple and functional; the material for the curtains might have been imported from Paris, but the space as a whole was imbued with a sense of organization and practicality. Her desk had been purchased for its usefulness as well as its appearance. And she did use it. She also used the computer that rested on it.

It was true that she had an agent and personal manager, a team of publicists and an assistant, but Chantel believed in keeping a handle on her own life, her own business. She knew what stocks she owned and the gross she received from the pictures she'd made. Copies of her contracts were meticulously filed. Chantel didn't simply sign them, she read them.

She went directly to her desk and, ignoring her thick appointment book and the pile of phone messages left by her maid, picked up a fat stack of papers. There were three scripts she hadn't so much as glanced at. The filming on *Strangers* wouldn't last forever. The sooner she started thinking about her next project, the less idle time she'd have.

Chantel got back into bed, propped the first script on her knees and told herself she would wait until eight o'clock for coffee. It only took half that time for her to discover that the first script was hopeless. The story itself had a few things going for it, but most of them were scenes with her naked, wrapped in one passionate embrace after another. She wasn't a prude, but neither was she willing to use her body as a selling point for a mediocre script. In any case, she was tired of playing the vamp or the victim. She tossed the script aside and picked up another. It caught her from the first page.

A comedy. At last someone had sent her an intelligent story that didn't rely exclusively on her sexuality to sell it. Not only was the dialogue sharp, the plot had twist after twist and made her chuckle out loud. The jokes were as much physical as verbal and would, she knew, exhaust her. Her character would make a fool of herself on-screen time after time. She'd end up with her face in the mud. And Chantel would love it.

Bless you, Matt. Halfway through the script, Chantel hugged it to her breast. He knew she wanted to do something at odds with the image they had both carefully created over the last six years. It would be a risk. Would people pay to see her face with mud on it? Chantel was willing to bet they would.

Happier than she'd been in weeks, Chantel pushed the intercom button and ordered breakfast brought up. She wasn't budging until she finished the last page. And when she did, she was going to call Matt. If she had to go to a casting call for this one, she would. If she had to read for the part, she'd read for it. She'd take a cut in salary if need be, but this was going to be hers.

Chantel snuggled back against the pillows, brought up her knees and turned the next page.

When the knock came at her door, she was totally absorbed. She answered absently, then began to chuckle as the character, *her* character, punched her way out of another crisis.

"Must be pretty funny stuff," Quinn commented.

Chantel's head whipped around. The amusement in her eyes turned instantly to annoyance. It was too bad, she thought, that he had to look so damn good. "A pity I didn't load that gun."

"You wouldn't shoot a man who's bringing you breakfast in bed." He moved across the room, set the tray on her lap, then made himself comfortable on the bed beside her. He wore a T-shirt and faded jeans and didn't seem to mind that his sneakers were on her handsewn spread. "What are you reading?" he asked, then stretched out his legs and crossed his arms behind his head.

"The stock market reports."

"Yeah, I always get a kick out of them, too." The pillows carried her scent, sexy, exotic and alluring. She was a bit rumpled from sleep, her hair tumbling around her shoulders and down her back. Even in the strong morning light he couldn't find a single flaw on her face. There were two skinny straps over her shoulders and a very little bit of lace low at her breasts. He remembered what he shouldn't have — what it felt like to hold her against him and kiss her until his mind went dim. He plucked a piece of toast off the tray and reached for the jelly.

"Help yourself," she muttered, fighting the urge to inch away.

"Thanks." He leaned over the tray as he

spread on a healthy portion of jelly. When his breath whispered warm over her bare shoulder, she stiffened and reminded herself how much she disliked him. "Like I said before, this is a great bed."

"When I get the bill for laundering the spread, I'll deduct it from your fee." Determined not to show any reaction, Chantel reached for the pot of coffee and poured a cup. "What can I do for you, Doran?"

He nibbled on the toast and just looked at her. The smile bloomed slowly, very slowly.

"Don't embarrass yourself," she told him, and sipped the coffee while it was too hot. When it scalded her tongue, she decided she didn't simply dislike him. She detested him.

"Ask a silly question," he began, then proceeded to pour himself a cup of coffee.

"Look, I'm busy, so if —"

"Yeah, I can see that."

"I happen to be reading some scripts."

"Any good?"

Chantel drew a deep breath. Some men were more thickheaded than others, she reminded herself. Perhaps if she humored him a little . . . "As a matter of fact, yes. I want to finish this one this morning, so if we've business to discuss —"

"You going to chew up another man in this one?"

Patience, Chantel told herself. It was compassionate to show patience to an idiot. "No. As it happens, this is a comedy."

"A comedy?" He let out one quick laugh before he drank. "You?"

Her eyes narrowed. "Don't push your luck, Doran."

"Come on, angel. Yours isn't the kind of face that a man pushes a pie into."

"It's mud."

"What?"

"In this case, my face gets pushed in mud."

He chose a piece of melon from her bowl. "That I'd have to see."

"I'm counting on several million people having your attitude." With a natural flair, she whipped the napkin from its ring and passed it to him. "You are, after all, the common man, aren't you?"

"As common as they come," he said easily.

"Now, why don't you tell me why you're here this morning with your feet on my bed and your hands in my breakfast."

"Just part of the service. Great coffee."

"I'll give your compliments to the chef. Now, why don't you get to the point?"

"Aren't you going to eat?"

"Doran."

"Okay." He took a small folder out of the side basket of the tray and opened it. "I have a couple of preliminary reports. Thought you'd be interested."

"Reports on what?"

"Larry Washington, Amos Leery, James Brewster. Also have a bit on the makeup guy and your driver."

"My driver? You're investigating Robert?" Her appetite gone, Chantel pushed herself farther up in bed. Quinn saw dark rose silk beneath the lace and wondered how far down it went. "That's the most ridiculous thing I've ever heard."

"Angel, don't you ever read mysteries? The one you least suspect is always the one who done it."

"I'm not paying you to play Sam Spade, and I'm damned if I can see paying you to run investigations on people like Robert and George."

After brief consideration, Quinn decided on a strawberry. "Have you ever noticed how your Robert looks at you?"

The lace rose up, then settled again with her breathing. Deliberately Chantel tilted her head. "Darling, *all* men look at me like that."

He gave her a long stare before he sipped his coffee again. Even he had problems separating her act from reality. "Since I have to start somewhere, I'm starting with the men closest to you."

"The next thing you'll tell me is you're investigating Matt." When he said nothing, she looked at him again. "You must be joking. Matt's —"

"A man," Quinn finished for her. "You just said that was all it takes."

Furious, Chantel picked up the tray, then dumped it in his lap. Coffee sloshed over the rims of the cups. "Look, let's just stop this right now. I'm not going to have people I care about spied on and embarrassed. Matt's the closest friend I have, and I was under the impression he was your friend, too."

"This is business."

"Let's say our business is concluded. The calls have stopped, and so have the letters."

"For a whole forty-eight hours."

"That's enough for me. I'll pay your fee through today, and we'll —" She broke off, the words sticking in her throat as the phone beside the bed began to ring. Without realizing it, Chantel found her hand in Quinn's, her fingers locked tight.

"They'll pick it up downstairs," he murmured. "Don't panic. If it's him, just keep calm. Try to get him to talk, to stay on the line as long as possible. We need time to run a trace." When the intercom buzzed, she jumped. "Pull yourself together, Chantel. You can handle it."

Working at keeping her breathing steady, Chantel spoke into the intercom. "Yes?"

"There's a man on the line, Miss O'Hurley. He won't give his name, but he says it's important. Shall I tell him you're unavailable?"

"Yes, I —" Quinn's hand curled around her wrist. "No, no, I'll take it. Thank you."

"Take it slow," Quinn told her. "Just let him talk."

Her fingers were stiff and cold as she picked up the receiver. "Hello." Quinn only had to look at her face to know she was hearing the familiar whisper.

"Don't lose it," he said quietly, keeping her free hand in his. "Just keep him on the line. Stay calm and answer him."

"Thank you," she managed, despite the block in her throat. "Yes, yes, I've gotten all your letters. No, I'm not angry." She closed her eyes and tried to pretend that the things he was saying didn't make her skin crawl. "I wish you'd tell me who you are. If you'd —" Caught between frustration and relief, she brought the receiver away from her ear. "He hung up."

"Damn." After setting the tray on the floor beside the bed, Quinn leaned over her and punched a few buttons on the phone. "It's Quinn." He swore again. "Yeah, just keep on it. Right. Not enough time," he told Chantel as he hung up the phone again. "Did he say anything that rang a bell, anything that makes you think of someone you know?"

"No." She trembled once before she regained control. "No one I know has a mind like that."

"Drink some coffee." He poured more into her cup, then handed it to her. She drank to ease the tightness in her throat.

"Quinn." She had to swallow again. "He said — he said he had a surprise for me, a big surprise." When she turned her head to look at him, her eyes were huge and dark. "He said it wouldn't be much longer."

"Let me worry about him." He'd always had a soft spot for the defenseless. It had gotten him into trouble before — in South America, in Afghanistan, and in countless other places. Even though he knew it might be dangerous in a more personal way, he slipped an arm around her shoulders and brought her close. "That's what you're paying me for, angel."

"He's going to get to me." She said it with such flat finality that he tightened his hold. "I can feel it."

"He'll have a hard time doing that with me in the way. Listen, I've got two men patrolling the grounds, two others monitoring the phones."

"It doesn't seem to help." She closed her eyes and for a moment let herself lean on him. "Maybe it's because I can't see them."

"You can see me, can't you?"

"Yeah." And she could feel him, could feel the hard, working muscles of his arm and shoulder, the not-so-smooth skin of his face.

"Want to see more of me?"

Cautious, Chantel lifted her face to look into his. There was humor there, but — she was sure she was mistaken — it looked as though there were genuine concern, as well. "I beg your pardon?"

"I like the way you do that. Angel, you could cut a man off at the knees without lifting a finger."

"It's a talent of mine. Explain, Doran."

"Why don't I move in for a while? Now don't let your ego get the best of you," he warned as she started to stiffen. "You've got plenty of rooms in this place, and though I am developing a real fondness for your bed, I can make do with another. What do you say, angel? Want a housemate?"

She frowned at him, hating to admit how much safer she would feel with him around all the time. The house was certainly big enough to keep them out of each other's way, though privacy would go out of the window. The real problem would be remembering just how he'd made her feel during that one sizzling kiss. If he were around twenty-four hours a day, remembering might not be enough.

"Maybe I should buy that vicious dog," Chantel muttered.

"Your choice."

That was true. It was. And she knew exactly how to handle it — and him. "Go ahead and get your duffel bag, Doran. We'll find a corner for you to sleep in." Sitting up, she flipped through the script again. She felt better, she couldn't deny it. The icy fist in her stomach had loosened. "How much extra is this going to cost me?"

"Meals — and I want more than a bowl of fruit in the morning — use of the facilities and, since this is going to play hell with my social life, another two hundred a day."

"Two hundred?" Chantel gave a quick, unladylike snort. "I can't imagine your social life's worth more than fifty. Isn't that the going rate in the massage parlors?"

"What do you know about massage parlors?"

She slanted him a look. "Just what I see in the movies, darling."

"How about a hands-on demonstration?" He lifted a finger and slid a strap from her shoulder. Instead of replacing it, Chantel simply studied the script.

"No, thanks. I doubt if there's anything you could teach me."

"I was thinking more the other way around." When he nudged the other strap aside, Chantel lifted her gaze to his. He was baiting her, and she wasn't ready to nibble.

"Try me when I've got a few weeks to spare, Doran. With you, I'm afraid we'd have to start from scratch."

"I'm a fast learner." He slid his hand up her shoulder until his thumb brushed her jaw.

She grabbed his wrist before she could stop herself, but her voice remained steady. "Watch your step."

"If you watch your step, you miss too much."

He'd wanted to touch her again, to feel her skin smooth and warm under his hands. He'd wanted to see her eyes darken, partly from anger, partly from temptation, when he did. She looked ready to rake his face, but the bite of her nails wouldn't stop him from sampling the fire she held so well banked inside her. The fire she let flame so explosively on screen.

When her free hand came up, he grabbed it. She held one of his, he held one of hers. As far as Quinn was concerned, they were even. He thought it was pride that kept her from struggling, pride and the confidence that she could bring him to his knees whenever she chose. He wasn't as certain as he wanted to be that she couldn't.

He was just about to let her go when her chin lifted and her eyes dared him. He'd always been a sucker for a dame.

With his eyes open and on hers, he lowered his mouth. But he didn't kiss her. Chantel felt the impact, both surprised and aroused, when he caught her bottom lip between his teeth. The chilly nonresponse she'd been determined to give him began to heat.

She could have stopped him. Her brother Trace had taught her and her sisters how to defend themselves from overamorous members of the male sex. Chantel was aware that she could take Quinn by surprise and have him bent over double and gasping for air with one quick jerk of her knee. She lay still, hypnotized by the green eyes that watched her.

She wasn't supposed to have these kind of feelings, this kind of hunger. She had blocked them out years before, when her emotions had made a fool of her. She wasn't supposed to have this slow, curling sensation in her stomach. Her bones weren't supposed to liquefy at a touch. She'd done love scene after love scene — choreographed, blocked out, shot and reshot for the camera — and had felt nothing that hadn't been programmed into her character. She knew just how little the most passionate embrace could mean to the two people involved.

This light, nibbling sensation on her lip should have done nothing but annoy her. But she lay still, trapped by an urgent desire to absorb the rushing range of feeling it brought to her.

Impossible. It had to be impossible, but he felt innocence shimmering around her. If it was an act, she was more skilled than she had a right to be. If it wasn't — but he couldn't think. She did something to his mind that she shouldn't be permitted to do. She pushed her way into it and filled it until he was ready to forget everything but her.

Desire. Desire was something easily quenched and easily forgotten. It would pay to remember that. Any man was bound to want her. But he wasn't sure any man would be able to forget her. There was too much power in her, the power to make a man hunger, to make him ache, to make him weak. Quinn couldn't afford to lose his hold. With her lips warm and soft under his, he reminded himself that he had two priorities. One was to keep her safe. The other was to look out for himself.

When he felt himself sinking, he pulled back. The ground was too unsteady here. For once he would indeed watch his step. "You pack a punch, angel."

Steady, she told herself, struggling to find a foothold. It meant nothing to him, nothing more than the eternal war of wills men and women fought. He hadn't gone soft inside or felt the need to be loved, the need to believe that maybe, just maybe, this was right. She wouldn't give him the satisfaction of knowing she had.

"Next time it'll flatten you."

"You might be right," he muttered, and shifted away. "Your skin's a little pale." He skimmed his gaze over her bare shoulders and cursed himself for the twist of need he felt. "Get dressed and meet me out by the pool. I'll bring you up to date on what we have so far." He rolled from the bed and, taking the file with him, left her alone.

He needed some air, fast.

★ ★ ★

Quinn cut through the water of the pool like an eel, smooth, fast and quiet. When Chantel came onto the path, she stood in the sunlight and watched him. She hadn't been wrong about the feel of his muscles. She could see them now, rippling with each stroke of his arm, bunching with each kick of his leg. He'd chosen brief black trunks from the stack she kept in the poolhouse for guests. They fit low and snug over his hips.

Still, she imagined he'd picked them for comfort rather than impact. As far as she could tell, Quinn Doran considered himself too irresistible to think about such things. She chose a chair by an umbrellaed table and waited for him to surface.

The physical exertion helped. Quinn realized he'd pushed himself closer to the limit with her than he'd intended. He still wasn't sure why he'd made a move toward her when he knew she was the kind of woman a smart man kept his distance from. He'd always been smart. That was the way you survived. But he'd also always had a habit of giving in to temptation. That was the way you lived. Though his life had never been dull, Chantel O'Hurley was his biggest temptation so far.

By the time he'd crossed the length of the

pool and back thirty times, most of the tension had drained. Under other circumstances he would have used a punching bag to relieve it, but he was willing to make use of whatever was available.

Tossing wet hair from his face, he stood in the shallow end, water lapping at his thighs. And he saw her.

Tipped back in the chair, her face shaded by a big, white umbrella, she was the epitome of cool, gut-wrenching beauty. She'd pulled her hair up and back so that her face was unframed. It needed no framing. The sleek, severe style only accented that fact. The snug top she wore was cut deep at the shoulders and cinched into the waistband of cropped shorts that showed off long, long legs. His gaze lingered on those legs as he hauled himself out of the pool.

"You've got a hell of a foundation, angel."

"So I'm told." Reaching beside her, she picked up a towel. "I see you're finding your way around all right." She tossed the towel to him, but he did no more than sling it around his neck. The sunlight shimmered on the drops of water on his bronzed skin.

"Nice pool."

"I like it."

"Then you should use it more. Swimming's a great way to keep in shape."

"I'll worry about my shape, Doran." Temper was licking its way to the surface. Chantel coated it with sarcasm. "Is this going to take long? I want to get my nails done this afternoon."

"We'll fit it in."

"We?" She couldn't prevent a smile as he sat across from her. "Somehow I can't picture you in a chi-chi little place like Nail It Down."

"I've been in worse." He shifted the chair slightly, placing himself in full sunlight. "Anything else on your agenda today?"

"Oh, maybe a little window-shopping on Rodeo Drive," she said on the spur of the moment, just to make things tougher. "Lunch at Ma-Maison, I think, or perhaps the Bistro." She rested her chin on the back of her hand. "It's been *days* since I've seen anyone. You do have something appropriate to wear, don't you?"

"I'll get by. Then there's that charity dinner tonight."

Her smile faded. "How did you know about that?"

"It's my job to know." Though he didn't need them Quinn flipped through his notes. "My secretary contacted Sean Carter and explained you had another escort."

"Then she can contact him again. Sean and I arranged to go together to help promote the film."

"Are you willing to get into a dark limo with a man who might be —"

"It's not Sean." After cutting him off, Chantel reached for the pack of cigarettes Quinn had tossed on the table.

"We'll just play this my way." Quinn picked up his lighter and flicked it on. "I'll take you to your little party, and if you like you can cuddle with Sean for the cameras. What about tomorrow?"

Chantel gave him a poisonous look. "You tell me."

Quinn patiently flipped open his file. "You've got a reporter and photographer from *Life-styles* coming at one to do a story on you and the house. That's all I've got."

She dropped the cigarette in an ashtray and let it smolder. "Because that's all there is. I have some personal things to attend to here at home, then I go to bed early because Monday's a working day."

"Matt said you were practical." Quinn flipped the page over. "Larry Washington."

"Get on with it," she told him. "You won't be happy until you do."

"The kid looks clean enough on the surface. Graduated UCLA last year with a degree in business management. Seems he always had a thing for the theater, but preferred the setups and backstage stuff to the acting."

"Which is exactly why I hired him."

"Apparently he had a pretty heavy thing going with a co-ed until about six months ago. A very attractive blue-eyed blonde. She dumped him."

He didn't have to spell out the implications. "A lot of women have blue eyes, and a lot of college romances break up."

"Amos Leery," he continued, ignoring her. "Did you know his first wife divorced him because he couldn't keep his hands off other women?"

"Yes, I know. And it was fifteen years ago, so —"

"Old habits die hard. George McLintoch."

"That's pitiful, Doran. Even for you."

"He's been a makeup artist for thirty-three years. Has five grandchildren and another due in the fall. Since his wife died a couple of years ago, he's had a few problems with the bottle."

"That's enough." She rose and paced to the edge of the pool. The water was calm and crystal clear. So had her life been only a few weeks before. "That's really enough.

114

I'm not going to sit here and listen to you dissect the personal problems of people I work with." She looked back over her shoulder. "You're in a filthy business."

"That's right." Not by a flicker did he reveal his feelings on the subject. "James Brewster. Seems like a pretty stable family life. Married twenty-one years, one son studying law in the east. Interesting that he's been in analysis for over ten years."

"Everyone in this town's in analysis."

"You're not."

"I will be if I keep you around."

He smiled briefly, then turned the page. "Your driver, Robert, is an interesting character. Young Robert DeFranco has himself a string of ladies."

"Just your kind of man."

"Can't help but admire his stamina. Matt Burns."

She turned all the way around then. This time he saw not anger but revulsion. It ripped at something inside him. "How could you?" She said it quietly and painfully. "He's your friend."

"This is my job."

"It's your job to spy into the personal lives of people you're supposed to care about?"

He kept his eyes on hers. "I can't afford to care about anyone but my clients when they're paying me. That's the service."

"Then keep this part of it to yourself. Whatever you dug up about Matt, I don't want to know."

He wouldn't allow her to make him regret what he'd done. He'd done worse, much worse. He wondered how she'd look at him if she knew. "Chantel, you're going to have to consider all the possibilities."

"No, *you* are. And at this point you're getting seven hundred a day to do it. It's your job to find whoever's hounding me and to keep me safe while you're doing it."

"This is the way I do it."

"Fine. Since it is, all I want to see from you is the bill."

She started to storm back into the house, but he blocked her path. "Grow up." Taking her by the shoulders, he held her still. She was hurting, he realized, really hurting for the people she cared for. He had to convince her that she couldn't afford to. "Anyone at all could be making those calls. Maybe it's someone you've never even met, but my instincts tell me different. He knows you, lady." He gave her a quick shake to accentuate his point. "And he wants you real bad. Until we find him, you're going to do just like I say."

That morning's call was still too fresh in

her mind. If a compromise had to be made, she'd make it. But she wouldn't like it. "I'll do what you say, Doran, to a point. I'll have my phone tapped. I'll have the damn guards at the gate and you in my house, but I won't listen to this garbage."

"In other words, you'll make a good showing, but you don't want the details."

"You got it."

He dropped his hands. "I thought you had more guts than that."

She opened her mouth to yell, then shut it again because he was right. She just didn't have the stomach for it. "Dry off, Doran."

She turned on her heel and walked away. As he stood watching her, Quinn decided his instincts were as reliable as ever. When push came to shove, she wouldn't crumble.

Chapter Five

When they got through the weekend without chewing any pieces off each other, Chantel decided they might make it. It hadn't pleased her to go to dinner with him and pretend, in front of three hundred other people, that she enjoyed being with him. Chantel had told herself to look at it as a job — a particularly difficult and unappealing job. Then Quinn had thrown her a curve. He'd been charming.

Surprisingly, black tie suited him. Though it didn't quite disguise his rough edges, it made them all the more appealing. He would never be suave or smooth or glossy. For some reason, Chantel found she was pleased to know that. He might wear a silk tie and the trappings of sophistication, but you knew — at least if you were a woman you knew — that a barbarian lay underneath.

Before the evening was over, he had drunk champagne with this year's top box-office draw and had danced with a three-time-Oscar-winning actress. The seventy-year-old veteran had patted Chantel on the knee and told her that her taste in men was improving. Though that had been difficult to swallow, not once during the evening had Quinn given Chantel the opportunity to smirk at him.

On Sunday he left her to herself. When the reporters came and she gave them an interview and a tour of her home, it was as if he weren't even there. She knew he was around, somewhere, but he didn't infringe on her privacy. She was free to get back to her reading, to indulge in a long, soothing whirlpool bath and to catch up on correspondence and a few niggling business matters. By the time they left the house on Monday morning, Chantel was almost ready to revise her opinion of him.

She felt rested and eager for work. The night before, she had finished the script she'd begun on Saturday morning and was more enthusiastic than ever. She'd woken Matt out of a sound sleep to tell him to go after the part. It might have been shy of 6:00 a.m., but Chantel felt wonderful.

She glanced over at Quinn beside her, legs stretched out, eyes closed behind tinted glasses. From the look of him, he hadn't shaved since Saturday. It seemed unfair that the slightly dissipated aura suited him so.

"Rough night?"

He opened one eye. Then, finding it too much effort, he closed it again. "Poker game."

"You played poker last night? I didn't know you'd gone out."

"In the kitchen," he muttered, wondering how soon he could get his hands on another cup of coffee.

"My kitchen?" Chantel frowned, a little annoyed that she hadn't been asked to play. "With whom?"

"Gardener."

"Rafael? He hardly speaks English."

"Don't have to to know a full house beats a straight."

"I see." A smile tugged at her lips. "So you and Rafael played poker in the kitchen, got drunk and told lies."

"And Marsh."

"And Marsh what?" She stopped in the act of reaching for a glass. "Marsh played cards? *My* Marsh?"

"Tall guy, not much hair."

"Really, Quinn, he's nearly eighty and quite creaky. I'm surprised even you would take advantage of him."

"Took me for eighty-three dollars. Canny old son of a —"

"Serves you right," she said with satisfaction. "Sitting down in my kitchen, swilling beer and smoking cigars and bragging about women when I'm paying for your time."

"You were asleep."

"I hardly think that matters. You're being paid to watch out for me, not play five-card stud."

"Five-card draw, jacks or better. And I was watching out for you."

"Really?" She brought a glass of juice to her lips. "That's odd. I didn't see hide nor hair of you yesterday."

"I was around. You enjoy your whirlpool?"

"I beg your pardon?"

"You spent damn near an hour in that tub." He took the glass from her and drained it. Maybe it would wash the cotton out of his mouth. "Funny, I figured a woman like you would have two dozen bathing suits. Guess you couldn't find one."

"You were watching me."

He handed the glass back to her, then settled back again. "That's what you're paying me for."

Indignation rippled through her as she slammed the glass back in its holder. "I'm not paying you to be a Peeping Tom. Get your prurient kicks on your own time."

"My time is your time, angel. I saw nearly that much of you when I plunked down ten bucks to see *Thin Ice*. Besides, if I'd been out for kicks, I'd have joined you."

"I'd have drowned you," she tossed back, but he only smiled and shut his eyes again.

His head was pounding like a jackhammer. He'd gotten less sleep before, but that had usually been of his own choosing. The poker game had been his way of distracting himself from the knowledge that she was sleeping upstairs, his way of trying to forget the way she'd looked stretched out in the foaming water of the spa that afternoon.

He hadn't, as he wanted her to believe, watched her. He'd seen her go into the poolhouse. Then, when she hadn't come out, he'd gone to check on her. She'd been lounging in the big tub, Rachmaninoff wafting from the overhead speakers. Her hair had been left down and floated in the frothing water. And her body . . . her body had been long and slender and pale. He could still feel the impact, like a sledgehammer straight to the solar plexus.

He hadn't stayed to tease and taunt, but had left as quietly as he'd come. There had been a fear, a definite fear that if she'd opened her eyes and looked at him he'd have crawled.

Thoughts of her haunted him day and night. He knew he should be able to prevent it. Nothing and no one was permitted to have power over him. But he was beginning to understand how a woman could become an obsession by simply existing. He was beginning to understand how a man could become overwhelmed by his own fantasies.

It made him worry about himself, but it made him worry more about her. If another man had become obsessed with her, and that other man had crossed certain lines, to what lengths might he go to have her? The letters and calls were gradually becoming more urgent. When would he stop them and try something more desperate?

As frightened as she was, Quinn didn't believe Chantel had any conception of just how far that kind of madness could push a man. The longer he was around her, the more he realized just how far that was.

They would shoot on the back lot that day. Another camera crew was already in New York filming exteriors. Chantel was looking forward to the time when she and other members of the crew would fly east for the handful of scenes to be shot on location.

It would give her a chance to see her sister Maddy and, with any luck, catch her play on Broadway.

The thought of it brought back her earlier cheerful mood. It lasted even through an hour's delay while technicians worked out a few bugs.

"Looks like New England," Quinn commented as he glanced around the open-air set.

"Massachusetts, to be exact," Chantel told him, nibbling on a sticky bun. "Ever been there?"

"I was born in Vermont."

"I was born on a train." Chantel broke off another piece of her bun and laughed. "Well, nearly. My parents were on their way to a gig when my mother went into labor. They stopped off long enough to have my sisters and me."

"Your sisters *and* you?"

"That's right. I'm the oldest of triplets."

"There are three of you. Good God."

"There's only one of me, Doran." She popped a piece of the bun in his mouth, enjoying the fresh air and sunshine. "We're triplets, but each of us manages to be her own person. Abby's raising horses and kids in Virginia, and Maddy's currently wowing them on Broadway."

"You don't look like the family type."

"Really." She felt too good to be offended. "I also have a brother. I can't tell you what he does, because no one's quite sure. I lean toward professional gigolo or international jewel thief. You'd get along beautifully with him." She watched one of the prop men pick up a boulder and move it a few feet. "Amazing, isn't it?"

Quinn studied the trees. They looked real, just like the ones back home, until you saw the wood base they sat on. "Anything real around here?"

"Not a great deal. Give them a few hours and they could make this a jungle in Kenya." Stretching her back, she toyed with the ice in her cup. She was used to waiting. "We were going to shoot this on location, but there were some problems."

"There's a lot of wait around in this business."

"It's not for the restless. I've gone back to my trailer and sat for hours to be called back for a five-minute scene. Other days you put in fourteen hours nonstop."

"Why?"

"Why what?"

"Why do you do it?"

"Because it's what I've always wanted to do." It was a stock answer. Why she felt obliged to elaborate on it, she didn't know. "When I was little and I sat in a theater and saw what could happen, I knew I had to be a part of it."

"So you always wanted to be an actress."

She tossed her hair back and smiled. "I've always been an actress. I wanted to be a star."

"Looks like you got what you wanted."

"Looks like," she murmured, shaking off a hint of depression. "What about you? Did you always want to be a — whatever it is you are?"

"I wanted to be a juvenile delinquent, and was doing a pretty good job of it."

"Sounds fascinating." She wanted to know more. To be honest, she wanted to know everything about him, but she'd take care how she asked. "Why aren't you serving ten-to-twenty in San Quentin?"

"I got drafted." He grinned, but she sensed the joke was very much his own.

"The army builds men."

"Something like that. Anyway, I learned to do what I was good at, make a profit and stay out of jail."

"And what are you good at?" He turned his head, just enough that she could see the amusement and the challenge in his eyes. "Forget I asked. Let's try something else.

How long were you in the army?"

"I didn't say I was in the army." He offered her a cigarette, then lighted it himself when she shook her head.

"You said you were drafted."

"I was. Drafted and government-trained. Want some more coffee?"

"No. How long were you in?"

"Too long."

"Is that where you learned not to give a direct answer?"

"Yeah." He smiled at her again. Then, before either of them realized his intention, he reached out to touch her hair. "You look like a kid."

Her heart shouldn't have been hammering, but it was. It was only a touch, after all, only a few words and a long look in a pretend world teeming with people. "That's the idea," she managed after a moment. "I'm twenty in this scene, innocent, eager, naive . . . and about to be deflowered."

"Here?"

"No, actually, just over there." She pointed to a small clearing in the forest the crew had created. "Brad the cad seduces me, promising me his everlasting devotion. He taps the passion that so far I've only given to my painting, then exploits it."

Quinn clucked his tongue. "With all

these people watching."

"I love an audience."

"And you got mad because I watched you in the tub."

"You —"

"They're ready for you, Chantel."

After giving her assistant a nod, Chantel stood up, then carefully brushed off the seat of her pants. "Get yourself a good seat, Doran," she suggested. "You might learn something."

Taking her advice, Quinn watched her run through the scene several times on low power. From his angle, it seemed a lukewarm stock scene — a gullible woman, a clever man in a pretty springtime setting. Plastic, he thought, pure plastic, down to the leaves on the trees. Quinn kept his eyes on George as the makeup artist retouched Chantel's face to keep that dewy, never-been-touched look intact. One of the prop men handed her back her sketchpad and pencil.

"Places. Quiet on the set." The hubbub died away, to be replaced by silence. "Speed. Roll film." The clapper came down for take 1. "Action."

It began the same way, with Chantel sitting on a rock sketching. Sean made his entrance and stood watching her for a moment. When Chantel glanced up and saw him, Quinn felt his mouth go dry. Everything a man could want was in that look. Love, trust, desire. If a man had a woman look at him that way, he could win wars and scale mountains.

He'd never wanted to be loved. Love tied you down, made you responsible to someone other than yourself. It took as much as or more than it gave. That was what he'd thought, that was what he'd been certain of, until he'd seen the look come into Chantel's eyes.

A movie, he reminded himself when he realized he'd missed five minutes of shooting. They were already doing a second take. The look in her eyes was as much an illusion as the forest they were in. And it hadn't been aimed at him, in any case. It was a movie, she was an actress, and it was all part of the script.

The first time Sean Carter touched her, Quinn felt his jaw lock tight. Fortunately for him, the director cut the scene.

When they continued, Quinn told himself he was under control. He told himself that he was only there because he was paid to be. She meant nothing to him personally. She was a case. It didn't matter to him how many men she made love with, on or off camera.

Then he watched her touch her lips softly, hesitantly, to Sean's, and he thought of murder.

It was only a scene in a movie, with fake rocks, fake trees and fake emotions. But it seemed so real, so honest. There were dozens of people around him with machines to run the lights, the mikes. Even as Sean gathered Chantel closer, a camera edged in on them.

But she trembled. Damn it, he saw her quiver as Sean pulled the band from her hair and let it tumble free. Her voice shook when she told him she loved him, she wanted him, she wasn't afraid. Quinn found his hands were balled into fists in his pockets.

Her eyes shut as Sean rained kisses all over her face. She looked so young, so vulnerable, so ready to be loved. Quinn didn't notice the camera come in close. He only saw Sean unbuttoning her blouse, and her eyes, wide and blue, locked on her lover's. Hesitantly she unbuttoned his shirt. Color washed her cheeks as she drew the shirt aside and pressed her cheek to his chest. They lowered to the grass.

"Cut."

Quinn came back to reality with a thud. He watched Chantel sit up, then say something to Sean that made him laugh. She was wearing a brief strapless bra that would stay below camera range and a pair of baggy jeans. Larry draped her discarded blouse over her shoulder, and she gave him an absent smile.

"Let's take it again. Chantel, after you take off his shirt, I want you to lift your head." Mary Rothschild hunkered down as Chantel rebuttoned her blouse. "I want a kiss there, a good long one, before you two go down on the grass."

Sometime during the fifth take, Quinn found his objectivity. He searched the faces of those looking on. If there was an uncomfortable stirring in his stomach, he could ignore it now. His job was to find out who might be watching Chantel, not clinically, not approvingly as she completed the scene, but someone who might be eaten alive with jealousy. Or fantasizing. It wasn't going to do either one of them any good if it was him.

Quinn took out another cigarette and watched the faces around him. He had reports coming in on everyone from the cinematographer to the prop man. Gut instinct told him that whoever was sending her letters was someone she knew, someone she might speak to casually every day.

Quinn wanted to find him, and he wanted to find him quickly. Before he developed an obsession of his own.

The assistant director put his arm around Chantel's shoulders and, with his head bent close to her ear, led her off the set. Before they reached the trailer that was Chantel's dressing room, Quinn was in front of them.

"Going somewhere?"

Chantel shot him a narrowed look but hung on to her temper. "As a matter of fact, I was going to get out of the sun for awhile. Amos was giving me the rest of today's schedule. You'll have to forgive Quinn, Amos. He's a bit . . . possessive."

"Hard to blame him." Good-natured and a bit tubby around the middle, Amos patted her shoulder. "You were terrific, Chantel, just terrific. We'll call when we need you for the close-ups and reaction shots. You should have about a half hour."

"Thanks, Amos." She waited until he was out of earshot before she turned on Quinn. "Don't do that."

"Do what?"

"All you needed was a knife between your teeth," she muttered, jerking open the door of the trailer. "I told you Amos was harmless. He —"

"Has a habit of touching women. One of those women is my client."

Chantel chose a diet drink from the small

refrigerator and collapsed with it onto the sofa. "If I didn't want him to touch me, I assure you, he wouldn't. This isn't the first time I've worked with Amos, and unless you insist on acting like an idiot, it won't be the last."

Quinn opened the refrigerator and, to his satisfaction, found a beer. "Look, angel, I can't narrow down the list of suspects to suit your requirements. It's time you stopped pretending that the person you're so afraid of isn't someone you know."

"I'm not pretending," she began.

"You are." He chugged back some of the beer before he sat beside her. "And you're not pretending with half as much style as you were out there rolling on the grass a few minutes ago."

"That's work. This is my life."

"Exactly." He took her chin in a way that made her eyes flash. "I'm supposed to take care of it. If it makes you feel better, I've just about eliminated Carter."

"Sean?" She felt a quick surge of relief, then one of caution. "Why?"

"Simple enough reasoning." He took another sip of beer and kept her hanging. "Seems to me that if a man was obsessed with a woman — We'll agree that we're dealing with an obsession?"

"Yes, damn it." She snatched the bottle out of his hand. "What are you getting at?"

"Just that if I were going over the edge about a woman I wouldn't be able to stand up, dust myself off and turn aside after I'd spent a good part of the day tangled half-naked with her."

"Is that so?" Chantel handed him back his beer. "I'll be sure to keep that in mind." Relaxed again, Chantel leaned back against the pillows and stretched out her legs. "So, what did you think of the scene?"

"It ought to fog up a few bifocals."

"Oh, come on, Quinn." She held up her drink and watched moisture bead the sides of the bottle. "It wasn't just a matter of sex, you know. It was a betrayal of innocence and trust. What happened to Hailey in that New England wood will affect the rest of her life. A quick tumble on the pine cones doesn't do that."

"But a quick tumble on the pine cones sells tickets."

"This is television. We're after ratings. Damn it, Quinn, I put a lot into that scene. It's the turning point of Hailey's life. If it doesn't mean more than —"

"You were good," he cut in, and had her staring at him.

"Well." She set her drink down. "Mind repeating that?"

"I said you were good. I don't hand out the awards, angel."

She brought her knees up and dropped her chin onto them. With the thin slash of sunlight coming through the curtains, she still looked young and innocent. "How good?"

"How do you manage to feed that ego when you're alone?"

"I've never denied the size of my ego. How good?"

"Good enough to make me want to give Carter a black eye."

"Really?" Delighted, she caught her bottom lip between her teeth. She'd play it light. It wouldn't do to let him know just how much it meant to her to hear him praise her work. "Before or after the cameras were rolling?"

"Before, during and after." Unexpectedly he reached over and took the front of her shirt in his hand. "And don't push your luck, angel. I've got a habit of taking what looks good to me."

"You've such class, Doran." She uncurled his fingers from her blouse. "Such low class."

"Just keep that in mind. You know, angel,

135

you gave me a twinge or two when I watched you and Carter paw each other."

"We weren't —"

"Give it any name you want. But good as you are, I didn't spend all my time watching you. I looked around and saw a few interesting things."

"Such as?"

"Brewster smoked a half a pack of cigarettes while you and Carter were . . . working."

"He's a nervous man. I've seen writers do worse when their script's being filmed."

"Leery practically fell in your lap trying to get a closer look."

"It's his job to look."

"And your assistant nearly swallowed his tongue when Carter took your shirt off."

"Just stop it." Springing up, she paced to one of the windows. They would call her soon. She wouldn't be any good if she let what Quinn was saying get her all churned up. "As far as I'm concerned, you're giving your own gutter-height views to everyone on set."

"That brings up another thought." He settled back and waited for her to look around at him. "Matt's yet to show up on the set. Strange. Aren't you his top client?"

She stared at him for a long moment.

"You're determined to leave me without anyone, anyone at all."

"That's right." He ignored the quick, bitter taste in his throat. "For the moment, you trust me and only me."

"They'll be calling me soon. I'm going to go lie down." Without looking at him again, she walked to the back of the trailer and through a doorway.

Quinn had a sudden fierce urge to throw the bottle against the wall. Just to hear it shatter. She had no business making him feel guilty. He was looking out for her. That was what he was paid for. And it was easier all around if she was suspicious. If that meant she shed a few tears, it couldn't be helped. He wasn't worried about it. He didn't give a damn.

Swearing, he slammed the bottle down on the table beside him. Lecturing himself all the way, he strode through the trailer to the bedroom. "Look, Chantel —"

She was sitting at the foot of the bed, staring down at an envelope in her hands. He smelled the dark, sweet scent of wild roses before he saw them on the dresser.

"I can't open it," she murmured. When she looked up at him, something twisted in his stomach. It wasn't just her pallor. It wasn't just the fear he could see in the way

137

her fingers shook. It was the complete and utter despair in her eyes. "I just can't take any more."

"You don't have to." With a compassion he thought had been erased in him years before, he sat beside her and gathered her close. "That's what I'm here for." He slipped the envelope out of her numb fingers. "I don't want you to open any more of the letters. If they come, you give them to me."

"I don't want to know what it says." She shut her eyes and hated herself for it. "Just rip it up."

"Don't worry about it." He stuffed the letter into his back pocket as he pressed a kiss to the top of her head. He had questions to ask, a lot of questions as to who might have gone into her dressing room that day. "Part of the deal is that you trust me. Just let me take care of things."

The head resting against his shoulder shook once in quick denial. "You can't take care of the way this makes me feel. I always wanted to be someone. I always wanted to feel important. Is that why this is happening?" With a dry sob, she pulled away from him. "Maybe you were right. Maybe I asked for this."

"Stop it." He took her hard by the shoulders and prayed she'd control the tears he could see were threatening. "I was out of line. You're beautiful, you're talented, and you've made use of it. That doesn't mean you're to blame for someone's sickness."

"But it's me that he wants," she said quietly. "And I'm afraid."

"I'm not going to let anything happen to you."

She let out a deep breath as her hand wrapped around his. "Sign that in blood?"

He smiled and ran a fingertip down her cheek. "Whose?"

Needing the contact, she rested her cheek against his for a moment. The gesture left him shaken. "Thanks."

"Sure."

"Look, I know I haven't been making this easy for you." She drew back again. As he'd hoped, the tears hadn't fallen. "I haven't wanted to."

"Trouble is my business. Besides, I like your style."

"While we're being nice to each other, I guess I'd say I like yours, too."

"A red-letter day," he murmured, and brought her hand to his lips.

It was a mistake. They both realized it the instant the contact was made. Over their joined fingers, their gazes met and held. She thought she could feel the tension jump from his palm to hers. This wasn't a matter of temptation, or of anger, or of passion flaring quickly, but of need. She needed to feel his arms around her again, holding her tight. She needed to feel his lips on hers, warm, hard, demanding. Everything else would fade, she knew, if only they came together now.

Their hands were still joined, but she didn't protest as his fingers tightened painfully on hers. What was he thinking? It suddenly seemed imperative that she understand, that she see, what he felt in his mind, in his heart. Did he want her, could he possibly want her as badly this moment as she wanted him . . . ?

No other woman had ever made him ache like this. Not just from wanting. No other woman had ever made his blood swim. Not just from looking. He thought it would be possible to sit there through eternity and just look at that face. Was it only her beauty? Could it possibly be that he was twisted around inside because of a flawless facade?

Or was it something else, something that seemed to glow from within? There was something elusive, almost secretive, that showed in her eyes only if you looked quickly and carefully enough. He thought he saw it now. Then all he could think of was how much he wanted her.

With his free hand he reached up to trail his fingers through her hair. Spun gold, like an angel's. That's what it made him think of. But she was flesh and blood. Not a fantasy, a woman. He leaned closer, then watched her lashes flutter down.

The knock on the trailer door had her shooting up like an arrow out of a bow. She put both hands to her face but shook her head when Quinn reached for her.

"No, it's all right. That's just my call to go on the set."

"Sit down. I'll tell them you're not feeling well."

"No." She dropped her hands to her sides. "No, this isn't going to interfere with my work." The fingers of her left hand balled into a fist, but he could see she was working to regain control. "I can't let that happen." Turning her head, she stared at the roses on the table. "I won't let it."

He wanted to overrule her but knew this was the one thing he'd admired about her from the first. She was strong, strong enough to fight back. "Okay. You want a few more minutes?"

"Yeah, maybe." She walked to the window and drew the curtains aside to let in more sun. It was frightening, much too frightening to think about darkness. At night she was alone with her thoughts and her imagination. The sun was out, she reminded herself, sighing deeply. She had work to do.

"Would you mind letting them know I'll be out in a minute?"

"I'll take care of it." He hesitated, wanting to go to her, knowing it would be a mistake for both of them. "I'll be right outside, Chantel. Don't come out until you're ready."

"I'll be fine."

She waited until she heard him walk away before she dropped her forehead onto the glass. Weeping would be such a relief. Weeping, screaming, just letting go, would ease the hammerlock her nerves had on her system. But she couldn't let go, any more than she could allow herself to get churned up like this. There were hours more to put in that day. She needed her wits, and her stamina.

She'd make it, Chantel promised herself. Drawing a deep breath, she turned from the window. The flowers were gone. She stared at the table with a foolish sense of relief. He'd taken them away. She hadn't even had to ask.

What kind of a man was he? Rude and rough one moment, tender the next. Why couldn't he be easy to understand and easy to dismiss? With a shake of her head, she started down to the front of the trailer. He was impossible to understand. And he stirred things in her. He was anything but the kind of man a woman could be comfortable with. And she felt so safe knowing he was close by.

If she hadn't known herself so well, been so certain of her own control, she would almost have believed she was falling in love with him.

Chapter Six

It was anything but a quiet, restful week, though Chantel spent a good chunk of it in bed. The bed was big and plush and ornate — and it was on the set, on soundstage D. The major scene to be shot was her wedding night — Hailey's wedding night — not to the man she loved but to the man she wanted to love.

The props included an ice bucket with champagne, a full-length sable draped over a chair and a table laden with roses that had to be spritzed constantly to keep them fresh under the lights. Don Sterling, a relative unknown, had been chosen to play the man she would marry. He'd been selected mainly because of looks and chemistry. Though his final reading with Chantel had been excellent, his nerves had him blowing the scene a half-dozen times during the morning.

Locked in his arms, Chantel felt him tighten up. Before he could do so himself, she flubbed the scene, hoping to take some of the pressure off him.

"Sorry." She gave a delicate shrug. "Can we take five, Mary? I'm getting stale."

"Make it ten," Rothschild ordered, then turned to consult with her assistant.

"How about a cup of coffee?" Chantel accepted the robe she was handed and slipped into it as she smiled at Don.

"Only if I can drown myself in it."

"Let's try drinking it first." She signaled to Larry, then found two seats in a relatively quiet corner. When she saw Quinn start to approach, she shook her head and leaned closer to Don. "It's a tough scene."

"It shouldn't be." He ran a hand through a mass of thick, dark hair.

"Look, the order they're shooting this miniseries in, we've only had a couple of scenes together so far. The first thing you know, we're married and on our honeymoon." She took the coffee from Larry. "I don't know about you, but I think it's easier to jump into bed with someone if you have more than a passing acquaintance."

He held the coffee in both hands and managed a chuckle. "I'm supposed to be an actor."

"Me too."

"You could run through this scene with your eyes closed." He sipped the coffee, then, with a sound of disgust, set it aside. "I'll be honest. You intimidate the hell out of me." When she only lifted a brow, he let out a long breath and looked away. "When my agent called and told me I had this part and that I'd be playing opposite you, I almost went into a coma."

"That makes it tough to work up any passion." She put a hand on his. "Look, your reading with me was great. No one else even came close."

"The bit in Hailey's art studio." He picked up his coffee with a rueful look. "Not a bed in sight."

"The first love scene I ever played was opposite Scott Baron. Hollywood legend — the world's sexiest man. I had to kiss him, and my teeth were chattering, I was so scared. He took me aside, bought me a tuna-fish sandwich and told me stories, half of which were certainly lies. Then he told me something true. He said all actors are children and all children like to play games. If we didn't play the game well, we'd have to grow up and get real jobs."

The tension she'd spotted around his mouth had already relaxed. "Did it work?"

"It was either that or the tuna fish, but we went back on the set and played the game."

"You stole that movie from him."

She smiled. "I've heard it said." She continued to smile as she sipped coffee. "Don't think I'm going to let you steal this one from me."

"You blew that last line on purpose."

She could become a prima donna with little more than a tilt of her head. "I don't know what you're talking about."

"You have a reputation for being cold and driven," he mused. "I never expected you to be, well, nice."

"Don't let it get around." Rising, she offered him a hand. "Let's get this honeymoon off the ground."

The scene went like clockwork. Quinn didn't know what Chantel had said during her brief huddle with her co-star, but it had turned the trick. For himself, he was learning not to tense up when Chantel was in someone else's arms. It was difficult to work up any resentment when so much technology went into setting the scene. The lights had to be adjusted to simulate candlelight. Chantel and Don lay in the bed, he stripped to the waist, she in a thigh-length chemise. The camera was nearly on top of them. The director knelt on the bed and went over the moves. On cue, Chantel and Don turned to each other as if they were the only two people on earth.

It was so easy for her, Quinn reflected, to fabricate passion. When he watched her like this, he wondered if she had any real feelings at all. Her emotions were turned off and on as direction indicated. Like an exquisitely crafted puppet, he thought, beautifully formed on the outside, hollow within.

Yet he'd held her himself. He'd felt passion shimmer in her. The feelings, needs, uncertainties had been there for him to touch. Had that been just part of her act, as well? It shouldn't matter to him, he reminded himself as he lighted a cigarette. He couldn't let it matter. She was an assignment and nothing more. If she stirred feelings in him, as she did with uncanny regularity, he would just have to take a step back. Involvement with a woman like Chantel O'Hurley was suicide for a man who didn't have himself under complete control.

But when he looked at her, his mouth went dry.

Just desire, he told himself. Or, more accurately, lust. There was no denying that wanting her was as easy, as natural, as drawing breath. But it hadn't been desire or lust he had felt when he'd held her in his arms moments ago.

So he had some compassion left in him.

Quinn found a chair, then discovered he was too wired to sit. He'd have been pretty low if he hadn't felt sympathy or been able to offer comfort to a frightened and vulnerable woman.

But it hadn't been sympathy, it had been rage. He recognized it even now, that hot, bubbling fury at the thought of his woman being threatened. His woman. That was the problem. The longer he was with her, the easier it became to think of her as his.

Take a step back from that, Doran, he ordered himself. And make it fast. If he didn't pull himself together soon, he was going to be in over his head. A man could only hold his breath for so long.

He crushed out his cigarette and wished the interminable day would end.

There had been two more letters that week, letters he hadn't shown her. The tone had shifted from pleading to near-whimpering. It worried Quinn more than the subtle menace the earlier letters had contained. The author was about to break. When he did, Quinn was certain it would be like a geyser, fast and violent. Because his own patience was thin, he hoped it would be soon. It would give him some outlet for the fury building inside him.

"That's a wrap, people. Don't have too

much fun over the weekend. We want you alive and coherent on Monday."

Still in her chemise, Chantel sat on the edge of the bed and held an earnest conversation with Don. Jealousy. Where it had come from and why, Quinn couldn't begin to answer. Quinn had always been a live-and-let-live sort of person. If a woman, even a woman he was involved with, decided to look to another man, that was her prerogative. No strings, no pain, no complications. He'd managed very well that way for years. He'd never experienced this sharp twist in the gut over a woman before. He felt it now, and he didn't like it, or himself. Unable to stop himself, he walked over and drew Chantel to her feet.

"Playtime's over," he said, and pulled her with him.

"Let go of me," she told him under her breath as he walked toward her trailer. Larry started forward with her robe, saw the look on Quinn's face and backed away.

"Just shut up."

"Doran, this is my place of business, but if you keep it up I'm going to create the biggest, juiciest scene even your twisted brain can imagine. You'll read about it in the paper for weeks."

"Go ahead."

She set her teeth. "Just what is your problem?"

"You're my problem, lady. For a woman who should be watching her step, you were awfully chummy with that kid."

"Kid? Don? For God's sake, he's an associate, and he's not a kid. He's two years older than I am."

"You were steaming up his contact lenses."

"Don't you get tired of playing the same tune?" She jerked her arm free and pulled open her dressing room door herself. "If you've been doing your job, you already have a report on Don Sterling and you know he's practically engaged to a woman he's been involved with for two years."

"And the woman in question is three thousand miles away in New York."

"I know that." As she pushed her hair out of her face the chemise shifted, whispering silkily over her skin. "He was just telling me that he's going to catch the red-eye to the east coast so that he can spend the weekend with her. He's in love, Doran, though I realize you might not understand the term."

"A man could be in love with another woman and still want you."

She slammed the trailer door and leaned back against it. "What would you know about love? What would you know about any genuine emotion?"

"You want emotion?" He slapped his palms on the door at either side of her head. Though her eyes widened in shock, she stood firm. "You want a taste of the kind of emotion you push out of a man? The real thing, angel, not something out of the pages of a script. Think you can take it?"

Her heart was beating in her throat. It was crazy to actually *want* to be dragged against him, to be plundered, drained and weakened. She could see nothing but raw fury in his eyes, but somehow she relished it. If it was all he could feel for her, it was almost enough. She'd be willing to settle, and that scared the hell out of her.

"Just leave me alone," she whispered.

"You're smart to be scared of me."

"I'm not scared of you."

He leaned a little closer. "You're trembling."

"I'm furious." She pressed her damp palms against the door.

"Maybe you are. And maybe that's because you're not quite sure of what happens next. It's not written out for you, is it, Chantel? Not so easy to turn the switch off and on."

"Get out of my way."

"Not just yet. I want to know what you feel." His body pressed lightly against hers. "I want to know *if* you feel."

She was losing ground, and what she had left was shaky. If he touched her now, really touched her, she was afraid she would lose everything. How could she tell him what she felt, when what she felt was against all the rules? She wanted to be held, protected, cherished, loved. If she told him that, he'd only smile and take what he wanted. She'd been left empty before, and it would never, never happen to her again.

Chantel lifted her chin and waited until his lips hovered an inch from hers. "You're no better than the man I hired you to protect me from."

He stepped back as if she'd slapped him. The stunned look on his face made her want to reach out to him. Instead, she pressed back against the door and waited for his next move.

"Get some clothes on," he told her, and turned aside. As she walked away, he reached into the refrigerator for a beer. She was right. Quinn twisted off the top and took two long swallows. He'd wanted to frighten, to weaken, then take her there, on his terms. If he could have proven to himself that what happened between them was cold and calculated, he might have believed she meant nothing to him.

He'd wanted to hurt her. She was threatening his peace of mind, and he'd needed to strike back. He would have used sex to purge himself and to repay her for the restless nights. The wave of self-disgust was as unfamiliar and as unpalatable as the surge of jealousy he'd felt earlier.

He'd told himself to take a step back, yet he'd taken a leap forward and had landed in the mire. He'd done things and seen things in his life that would have left others pale and speechless. Yet, for the first time in his life, he felt truly soiled.

When he heard her coming back, he tossed the bottle into the trash. She wore rose-colored linen slacks and a jacket with a muted floral design. She looked cool, composed and nothing like the restless, questing character she'd played all day.

Without a word she walked by him and put her hand on the knob. Before she could open the door, Quinn placed his hand over hers. He cursed himself when she stiffened and sent him a cool, disinterested look.

"You're entitled to take a few shots," he said mildly. "I won't even duck."

For a moment she said nothing. Then, as the anger dissipated she sighed. She was tired, drained from the constant play and replay of emotion. "I'll take a rain check."

As she twisted the knob, he tightened his hand on hers. "Chantel . . ."

"What?"

He wanted to apologize. It wasn't his style, but he wanted badly to tell her he was sorry. The need was there, but the words wouldn't come. "Nothing. Let's go."

They rode home in silence while guilt ate at him. It would fade, he assured himself. It was just one more of the odd emotions she drew out of him. She looked exhausted now, though he remembered she'd looked fine — in fact, she'd looked wonderful — before he'd . . .

Damn it, he couldn't waste his time worrying about things like that. He had a job to do, and if he'd stepped out of line, it wouldn't happen again. Case closed. He'd see her into the house, make certain the doors were locked and the alarm on. Then he'd relax. He needed to go over the report from his field man, though he was already aware they'd turned up nothing on the stationery. They needed a mistake. So far, no matter how mentally unstable Chantel's admirer was, he'd been smart.

Quinn sat back as the limo cruised through the gates, wishing he could say the same thing about himself.

He preferred to act on impulse. As he stepped out of the car, he didn't hesitate or think twice. Taking Chantel by the hand, he began to lead her around the side of the house.

"What are you doing?"

"It's Friday night and I'm sick of being cooped up in that house. We're going out to eat." He stopped by his car and nodded to one of the men who patrolled the grounds.

"Did it ever occur to you that I might not feel like going out?"

"Where I go, you go." He opened the door and started to nudge her inside.

"Doran, I've put in sixty hours this week and I'm tired. I don't want to go to a restaurant and be stared at."

"Who said anything about a restaurant? Just get in, angel. You don't want to embarrass yourself in front of my man over there."

"I'm not hungry."

"I am." He gave her a quick shove, then shut the door behind her.

"Has anyone ever mentioned that you're totally lacking in manners or any of the other social graces?"

"Constantly."

He gunned the motor and sent the car barreling down the drive. Chantel reached for her seat belt. "If you wreck this heap with me in it, the producers are going to have your head on a platter." For a moment she wondered if it wouldn't be worth it.

"Nervous?"

"You don't make me nervous, Doran, you simply annoy me."

"Everyone's got to be good at something." He turned the radio dial, and loud, throbbing rock poured out. Chantel closed her eyes and pretended to ignore him.

When the car came to a halt, she didn't move. Determined to show nothing but indifference, she sat still as the silence grew. Outside the car she heard the bump and grind of weekend traffic heating up. She had no idea where they were and told herself she didn't care. Quinn's door opened and closed, and she still didn't move. But she did open her eyes.

She saw him stride up to the little fast-food joint and fought back a chuckle. She would not be amused. At home she could have had a nice glass of wine and a crisp salad with her cook's special herb dressing. God knew what Quinn was carrying back to the car in the white bag. She simply wouldn't eat, she told herself. She'd let him get whatever he had in his system out, but she wouldn't eat.

Closing her eyes again, she tried not to react as aromas, really wonderful aromas, filled the car. He glanced over, smiled, then started the car again.

Again she didn't know where he was heading, but the road began to wind and the sounds of traffic faded. She very nearly dozed off as her system absorbed the quiet sunset drive. She hadn't realized how much she'd needed to get away, from work, from her house, maybe from herself. It was going to be hard not to be grateful to him. But Chantel told herself she would manage.

When the car stopped again, she refused to move. Curiosity gnawed at her, but she kept her eyes firmly shut. Saying nothing, Quinn reached for the bag, rattling it so that the scent seeped through the car. Then he stepped out and closed the door behind him.

Chantel's stomach contracted, reminding her that the plate of fruit and cheese she'd had for lunch wasn't enough. The least he could do was force her to eat something, the way he'd forced her to do other things she hadn't wanted to. But no, she thought as her temper began to rise, he would just go off and gobble up whatever was in that bag and let her starve.

Opening her eyes, Chantel pushed open

her door. As she let it slam behind her, the noise seemed to echo forever. Astonished, she looked around her.

They were farther up in the hills than she had ever gone before. Below, miles below, L.A. stretched forever, glistening just a bit as lights winked on. She could see the separate levels of color in the sky as the sun went down. Deep blue led to paler blue, and paler blue to mauve and rose and pink, all glistening with gold. The first star blinked to life overhead and waited patiently for others to join it. The breeze whistled through the brush, but the city she knew so well seemed encased in glass, it was so quiet.

"Pretty impressive, isn't it?"

She turned and saw Quinn leaning against a giant H. The Hollywood sign, she realized, and nearly laughed. She'd seen it so often it no longer registered. From the hills it looked white, invulnerable and perhaps immortal. Up close, like the town it heralded, it was mostly illusion. It was big and bold, certainly, but a little grimy, a little shaky. Graffiti was etched in clumps near the base.

"It could use a fresh coat of paint," she murmured.

"No, it's more honest this way." He

kicked aside a beer can. "Teenagers come up here to hang out — and make out."

She tilted her head. "And you?"

"Oh, I just like the view." He climbed over a few rocks effortlessly and planted himself on the base of an L. "And the quiet. If you're lucky, you can come up here and not hear a thing, except for a coyote now and again."

"Coyote?" She glanced over her shoulder.

"That's right." Not bothering to hide a grin, he dug in the bag. "Want a taco?"

"A taco? You dragged me all the way up here to eat tacos?"

"Got some beer."

"Lovely."

"It's getting warm. You'd better drink up."

"I don't want anything."

"Suit yourself." He unwrapped a taco and bit into it. "Got some fries, too," he said with a full mouth. "A little greasy, maybe, but they're not cold yet."

"I don't know how I can resist." She turned away from him to look down at the city again. As fate would have it, the breeze carried the spicy scents to her. Her mouth watered. Chantel scowled down at the lights and wished Quinn Doran to hell.

"I guess a woman like you turns her nose

up if it isn't champagne and caviar."

Spinning around, Chantel stood with the city and the sunset at her back. Quinn felt his heart turn over in his chest. She'd never looked more beautiful. "You know nothing about me, nothing at all." Her voice had an edge to it now, a dull, gritty edge that had his eyes narrowing. "I spent nearly the first twenty years of my life shuffling from town to town, eating in greasy spoons or over a hot plate in a motel room. Sometimes, if we were lucky and the gig was good, we got to wolf down a meal in the hotel kitchen. If we weren't so lucky, there were always hard-boiled eggs and coffee. Don't you sit there in your smug little world and toss stones at me, Doran. You don't know what I am, or who I am. All you know is what I've made myself."

Slowly he set the beer on the rock behind him. "Well, well," he said quietly. "I wouldn't read any of that in your official bio, would I?"

She could only stare. What was it about him that made her lose control? Why had she been compelled to yank herself out and expose her roots to him?

"I want to go back."

"No, you don't." His voice wasn't curt now, but gentle. It was that gentleness that chipped away her defenses. "There's no one here but me, Chantel. Why don't we just sit up here and look down at the rest of the world for a while?"

Before she'd thought it through, she'd taken a step toward him. When he rose and held out a hand to help her up, she reached for it without hesitation. Hesitation came the moment his palm met hers. She remembered the feel of it, the strength of it, and her gaze lifted and locked with his. They stood there a moment with the sky darkening around them. Then he hauled her up.

"I'm sorry." The apology surprised him as much as it did her.

"For what?" She started to draw her hand from his, but he reached up to brush back her hair.

"For what happened before. I don't know why, but something about you makes me edgy."

She kept her eyes level with his. "Then we're even."

The wind tossed the hair back from his face. In every situation, he knew, there came a time for honesty. Perhaps this was such a time. "Chantel, I want you. I'm having a hell of a time dealing with that."

Other men had wanted her, other men had told her so in more beautiful ways. But the words had never made it difficult for her to breathe. "I could fire you."

"It wouldn't matter."

"No, I don't suppose it would." She looked away, surprised at how strong a longing could be. "Quinn, I can't go to bed with you."

"I figured you'd feel that way."

"Quinn." She took his hand again as he started to step away. "I don't know what you think my reasons are, but I guarantee you, you're wrong."

"Not your style," he said, picking up his beer again. "Not your league."

Chantel snatched the bottle from him and heaved it. Spray spewed against the rocks before the glass shattered. "Don't tell me what I think. *Don't* tell me what I feel."

"Then you tell me." He grabbed her and pulled her against him.

"I don't have to tell you *anything*. I don't have to explain myself to you. Damn you, I just want some peace. I just want a few hours where the pressure's off. I don't know if I can take being squeezed at all sides for much longer."

"Okay, okay." His hold gentled immediately. As he murmured, his hand stroked up and down her back. "You're right. I didn't bring you up here to fight with you, but you make me edgy."

"Let's just go back."

"No, sit down. Please," he added, brushing his lips over her hair. "Let's see if we can stay here for an hour together and not pick on each other. Have a taco."

He smiled at her as he pulled her down to sit. Chantel took one look at the bag and gave up.

"I'm starving."

"Yeah, I figured as much." He handed her a wad of paper napkins. For the next few minutes they ate in companionable silence. "Was your childhood rough?"

Chantel stopped in the act of opening a little packet of salt for the fries. "Oh, no, I didn't mean that. It was just different. My parents are entertainers. They've been a song-and-dance team for over thirty years. The six of us trouped around the country, and some of the places we played were dives. But my family . . ." She smiled, absently accepting a beer. "They're wonderful. Trace did some routines, but he was best on the piano. It always used to frustrate me that no matter how hard I tried I couldn't play better than he did."

"Sibling rivalry."

"Sure. Life would be pretty dull without it. Trace and I were always so much alike that we couldn't stay off each other's backs for very long. There was never much of that between my sisters and me. We were just too much a part of each other." She sipped the beer straight from the bottle and looked down at the city below. "We still are. God, sometimes it's so hard to be away from them. When we were little we made all these plans for keeping the act together forever." She remembered them with a little pang of regret. "Then we grew up."

"What kind of an act?"

Laughing, she licked salt from her fingers. "You never heard of the O'Hurley Triplets?"

"Sorry."

"You'd probably be sorrier if you had heard of us. Three-part harmony, show tunes and popular music, a few old standards thrown in."

"You sing?"

"Doran, I don't just *sing*. I'm terrific."

"You never sing in your movies."

She shrugged a shoulder. "It hasn't come up. Matt keeps saying we should give the public a surprise one of these days and get a guest spot where I can do a few numbers, and dance, maybe too. Yes," she added when he slanted a look at her, "I can dance — my father would have died of shame otherwise."

"Why don't you do it?"

"The time just hasn't been right. Besides, I've been concentrating on what I'm best at."

He balled up the empty bag and set it beside his feet. "What's that?"

She gave him a quick, mocking look. "Playing roles."

Instead of smiling back, he tucked her hair behind her ear. "My guess is you're not playing one now."

She turned her head quickly and looked out. The sky was nearly dark, but there was only a smattering of stars. "You can't be sure. I'm not sure myself half the time."

"I think you're sure."

When she turned her head back, his mouth was close. Close and tempting. "Don't. I told you I can't —" But his lips brushed over hers, light as a whisper, and stopped her cold.

"Do you know how I felt when you were lying on that bed with Sterling today?"

"No. I don't want to know. I've told you, it's my job."

She was already half seduced; he could hear it in her voice. There was a thrill of anticipation along his skin as he thought of taking her beyond the next step. "I wasn't sure if I wanted to put my hands around his throat or yours, but I did know I wanted you to look at me the way you were looking at him."

"It's just a part. I'm supposed to —"

"There aren't any cameras here, Chantel. Just you and me. And that's what I think you're afraid of. No one's here to tell you what you're supposed to be feeling. No one's going to yell 'Cut' before things go just a little too far."

"I don't need anyone to tell me what to feel. I don't need anyone," she repeated, and tugged his mouth back to hers.

She wanted it. She wanted to experience the wild flood of sensation he could bring her. No one else. She could tell him there'd been no one else who had touched her just this way, but he'd never believe her. The image, her image, was all but carved in stone, and she'd polished it herself. What she was inside belonged to her. She was determined that no one would ever share that part of her again.

But she could have this, the heat, the need, the desperation. She could take this, and she could give it back to him as long as she promised herself she wouldn't give him too much. As long as she didn't give him everything.

The sky darkened above them, and the wind whistled through the brush.

She was pulling something from him, drawing something out of him. He couldn't seem to stop her. His hands weren't steady as they reached up to tangle in her hair. His mind was swimming in a mist of his needs, but the needs weren't as simple as he'd told himself they had to be. Desire could make you ache, but it shouldn't be allowed to slice you open.

He wanted to take her there, there in the rocks and dirt. He wanted to treat her like porcelain, delicately and with intense care.

His body was coiled tight, ready to explode. God, he had to touch her, even if it was only once. In one smooth stroke he brought his hand along her leg, over her hip, until he found and cupped her breast. She was small, incredibly fragile, and as soft as water. Compelled, he flicked open the two buttons on her jacket to feast on the warm flesh inside.

It had been so long, so long since she had allowed herself to be touched, since she'd felt the need for intimacy. She wanted his hands on her, his lips on her, his body hard and demanding against hers. The hell with where they were, who they were. The hell with the price she would surely pay for allowing herself to love him.

In an act of surrender that left him

shaken, she brought her arms around him and buried her face against his throat.

"Chantel . . ." He started to tilt her face up, longing, for reasons he couldn't be sure of, to see what was in her eyes. Then he heard it, a rustling in the brush that came once, then twice, and had him tensing.

"What? What is it?" She had heard it, too, and she dug her fingers into his arm. "An animal?"

"Yeah, probably." But he didn't think so. His nerves were humming as he drew her aside.

"Where are you going?"

"To take a look. Just stay here."

"Quinn —" She was already standing.

"Just sit tight. It's probably just a rabbit."

It was no rabbit. She heard it in his voice. He wasn't nearly the actor she was. Fear made her want to cringe away. Pride had her matching him step for step. "I'm going with you."

"Chantel, sit down."

"No." She held his arm and scrambled over the rocks.

Resigned, Quinn helped her regain her balance. "All right, then, be careful. You get any scratches on that skin and I'll get blamed for it."

"Damn right."

Because the light had faded, he went to his car and found a flashlight. "Why don't you just sit —"

"No."

Swearing under his breath, he took her by the arm again. He walked slowly toward the brush, casually angling his body to shield hers. "Lot of game up here," he began, but his muscles were coiled and ready. He moved softly, quietly pushing brush aside as Chantel hung on to his hand.

"I remember, coyote."

"Yeah." He crouched down when he spotted prints in the soft dirt. The beam of his light swept over them, then held.

Chantel pressed her lips together. "I guess coyote don't wear shoes."

"None that I've seen." He hated hearing that hint of fear in her voice. "Look, it was probably just a kid."

"No. You don't believe that and neither do I." She stared down at the scuffed prints. The brush where they were wasn't more than five yards from where they'd been sitting a moment before. "Someone was watching us, and I think we both know why. God." She pressed her fingers to her eyes. "He was here. He was right here, just watching. Why doesn't he stop? Why doesn't he —"

"Get a hold of yourself." Quinn took her

by the shoulders and shook. She took a deep breath, then nearly screamed when the sound of an engine starting echoed back to them.

"He followed me." She stopped trembling. Her body felt too numb even for that. "How many other times has he been there, watching me?"

"I don't know." Frustrated, Quinn stared out at the darkening road. Even if he dared leave her there alone, he'd never catch up with the other car now. "Just remember, he's watching us now. I'm not going to let him get to you."

"For how long?" she said quietly, then turned away. "I want to go back."

Chapter Seven

"It just doesn't seem like we're getting anywhere." Chantel poured herself a brandy, then freshened Matt's glass.

"I'm sorry, Chantel. I'd have sworn if anyone could dig up an answer it would be Quinn."

"I'm not blaming him." Cupping her brandy in both hands, she walked to the window. The sun was setting. It reminded her of another dusk. With the snifter at her lips, she watched night fall.

"You've changed your tune from the first time we talked about him."

More than you know, she thought, but shrugged her shoulders. "I can't claim he's not doing everything he can, that's all."

"Then maybe I have to," Matt returned, hating to hear the tired resignation in her voice. "He hasn't come up with anything solid. What about the letters?"

"The stationery the letters were written on could have come from any of dozens of dollar or drugstores in the L.A. area.

There's no way for him to trace it."

"But the flowers." Restless, Matt walked to the white baby grand, then back to the fireplace, his cigarette trailing expensive smoke behind him. "There has to be a way to trace where they were bought."

"Apparently not. Most of the time they just appear in my dressing room or somewhere on the set. So far no one's seen who delivers them."

"Florists keep records."

"If you pay cash and pick up the flowers yourself, there wouldn't be any reason to ask for ID." She pressed her fingers to the back of her neck, pressed and released, fruitlessly working at a knot of tension.

"Someone might remember who —"

"Quinn tells me his men have done a sweep of the florists in the area. There's nothing."

"The phone calls."

"They haven't been able to get a trace."

"Damn it." If something — or someone — existed, Matt felt there must be a way to find him. "Chantel, maybe you should reconsider the police."

She turned back. With him, she could allow the weariness to show. "Matt, do you really think they could do more than Quinn's done?"

"I don't know." The quiet desperation in her eyes was difficult to face. He scowled down at his brandy. "I just don't know." Setting down his drink, he crossed to her. "I was sure this thing would be tied up in a matter of days."

"It's not as simple as that. It seems he's clever, or cautious, at any rate."

"Are you sure you've told Quinn everything you know?"

"What I don't tell him, he finds out." Nerves had her swirling the brandy around and around in her glass but not drinking. "He's running investigations on everyone I know."

"Well, that —"

"Including you."

He stopped to stare at her. With a grimace, he stuck his hands in his pockets and nervously pulled out his lighter. "He's thorough, anyway."

"I don't like it, Matt." For the first time, real emotion came into her voice, into her eyes. "I feel . . . I don't know, sleazy when I think of him poking into the keyholes of people's lives, and on my account."

Not quite comfortable. Matt slipped an arm around her shoulder. "Look, baby, if rattling a few skeletons in my closet helps get to the bottom of this thing, then it's worth it." He was silent a moment, then cleared his throat. "So, what did he find out?"

"About you?"

"That's a good place to start."

"I don't know." Letting out a long breath, she leaned her head on his shoulder. The sun had disappeared completely, leaving only a hint of color streaking the clouds. "I told him I didn't want to know, Matt. He started to give me reports on people like Larry and James Brewster, and I hated it." She could still remember his cool disapproval of her cowardice. Chantel gritted her teeth against the memory. "We agreed that I'd take the precautions he'd outlined, and that he'd keep what information he had to himself."

With one hand he flicked on the silver monogrammed lighter he'd been toying with. "That's burying your head in the sand, Chantel."

"I don't care."

"Listen, there's no one, certainly no one who's made it past twenty, who hasn't done something they're ashamed of, something they'd prefer to keep covered." He shifted but made himself speak matter-of-factly. "Quinn's got a right to investigate, and because of who he is, nothing he finds out would go any farther."

"Thanks for the vote of confidence." Quinn paused in the doorway and studied them. Matt still had his arm around her. Chantel's head rested on his shoulder as the dim light through the window behind them settled over her hair. She looked comfortable with him, Quinn realized with a twinge of resentment. She looked as though she'd be content to snuggle up against him and sit for hours.

"I'm the one who recommended you," Matt said easily. "I'd hate to say I'd made a mistake."

"You didn't." Quinn crossed to the bar to pour himself a double shot of brandy. "How've you been, Matt? I thought we'd be seeing more of you."

"I've been tied up."

Sensing the restraint between them, Chantel took a step forward. "Just stop it," she told Quinn. "Don't start on him."

"You're telling me how to do my job again, angel."

"I'm not going to allow you to use your third degree on my friends."

Quinn tossed back his brandy. "Too bad I left my rubber hose upstairs."

"Why don't we sit down?" Matt put a hand on Chantel's shoulder. "I appreciate it, babe, but it isn't necessary." His gaze locked with Quinn's. "I guess when I told Chantel to hire you I should have figured you'd dig it up."

Quinn met the look, but there was nothing to show his feelings. "Yeah, you should have."

"Dig what up?" she demanded.

Quinn lifted his glass in a half salute. "Maybe you'd like to tell her yourself."

"Yes, I would. Sit down, Chantel." When she only looked at him, Matt squeezed her shoulder. "Please, sit down."

She felt the now-familiar churning in her stomach as she chose a chair. "All right, I'm sitting."

"A few years back, almost ten now, I ran into some financial problems." He retrieved his brandy and took a deep swallow.

"Matt, you don't have to tell me about this."

"Yes, I do." He looked back at Quinn. "I want you to hear it from me." He held up a hand before she could protest again. "Just hear me out. When I'm finished maybe I won't feel as though the blade's about to fall on my neck."

"All right," she said evenly, but her left hand moved restlessly on the arm of her chair.

"Gambling," he said with a hint of fear in his voice.

"Matt, that's absurd." She nearly laughed. "You won't even play gin for matchsticks."

"That's now. This was then. I couldn't keep away from the horses." With a self-mocking smile, he looked back at her. "It's a fever, and mine ran pretty hot until I'd dropped more than I could afford. I was desperate. I'd borrowed money from a certain group of people — the kind who break small bones in your body if they don't get their weekly payment."

"Oh, Matt."

"I needed ten thousand I didn't have. I forged a check. A client's check." He closed his eyes before he took another swallow. Chantel sat in silence. "Of course, it didn't take long for it to come to light. My client didn't want the publicity, so he didn't press charges. I mortgaged my soul, then hocked the rest to pay him back. You could call it a turning point in my life." This time he laughed, but there was no humor in it. "My career was on the line, so I took a good hard look at myself. Because what I saw left me pretty shaken, I checked into an organization for obsessive gamblers. It's been nearly eight years since I've been to the track. Even though gambling nearly ruined my life, I have to fight the urge every day to place just one bet." He set down his glass and looked at her. "If you want another agent, I'll understand."

She rose slowly and walked to him. Without a word, she put her arms around him and gathered him close. Over his shoulder she sent Quinn a long, neutral look. "I don't want another agent. You know I insist on the best."

With a muffled laugh, he pressed a kiss to her brow. "You're a special lady."

"Someone's always telling me that."

He gripped her fingers hard, and she felt how damp his palms were. "I wouldn't let you down, Chantel."

"I know."

He kissed her again before he drew away. "I've got to get going. You'll call if there's anything I can do?"

"Of course."

He turned to Quinn. For a moment the men studied each other across the room. If there was regret on either side, they didn't show it. "Take care of her."

"I intend to."

With a brief nod, Matt let himself out.

Chantel turned on Quinn immediately. "How could you? How could you humiliate him that way?"

"It was necessary." But necessary or not, it left a foul taste in his mouth. Quinn poured another brandy, knowing that taste wouldn't be so easily washed away.

"Necessary? Why? What does a gambling debt nearly ten years ago have to do with what's happening to me now?"

"If a man can develop one obsession, he can develop another."

"That's ridiculous."

"No, that's a fact."

A quiver ran through her, not of fear but of anger. "Matt Burns has never attempted to be anything to me other than my agent and my friend. And he's had abundant opportunity."

"Would you have let him?"

Chantel took a cigarette, then flicked the table lighter three times before she managed to get it to flame. "What does that have to do with it?"

He came closer, curling his hand firmly around her arm. "Would you?"

"No." Tossing her head, she blew out smoke. "No."

"And he knows it." When she jerked her arm away, he watched her pace the room. "You're good with scenarios. Try this one. The man works with you for years, he watches you soar straight to the top. He's helped you, layer by layer, to build that illusion of cool, ice-hard sexuality. Maybe he wants what he helped to create."

A shiver ran down her spine, but her eyes were calm and level when she turned to him. "It doesn't play, Doran."

"It plays as well as anything else."

"No, it doesn't." The fear was back. She fought hard to keep it from showing. "Why wouldn't a man I know, a man I'm close to, just approach me openly?"

"Because he's a man you know, a man you're close to," Quinn countered. "He knows he doesn't have a chance with you on that level."

Impatient, she stubbed the cigarette out. "How would he know if he's never asked?"

Quinn put a hand to her cheek to stop her nervous pacing. "Don't you think a man knows when a woman's interested?" Running a thumb down her jaw, he brought her an inch closer. It was there, as it had been from the first, humming between them. She felt it, damn it, he knew she felt it, even though she refused to show that she did. "Don't you think he can look at a woman, see the way she looks at him, and know if they're going to be lovers?"

She put a hand to his wrist and carefully

drew his away. Her skin felt as though it would stay warm for hours. "I'm tired," she told him. "I'm going to bed."

When he was alone, the brandy tempted him. Because it seemed too easy a way out, he turned his back on it. He went outside to walk the grounds.

Chantel was finding sleep harder and harder to come by. In the late hours she would toss and turn, then fall into a light doze, only to awake again, nervous and groggy, to toss and turn some more. Several times she had been tempted to give in and get a prescription for sleeping pills. Each time she remembered her promise never to tranquilize herself against pressure, personal or professional.

She thought of Matt, of the self-disgust and apology in his voice as he'd told her something she had no business knowing.

She thought of Quinn, firm and unyielding but offering Matt the chance to explain for himself.

Oddly enough, she thought of her brother and an argument they'd had when she'd been a teenager. Trace had threatened to knock some boy's block off if he got too familiar with her. Chantel remembered being furious at him for interfering, and telling everyone she could handle things.

Why wasn't she in control now?

She always had been. Even Trace had known then she hadn't needed him to stand up for her. Perhaps because she'd been one of three in the womb, she'd been born ready to handle her own problems. She'd faced tragedy, personal loss and disillusionment but had always managed to fight her way back. She wasn't fighting now, and she should be. It had never been necessary for her to look to a man for protection, and yet . . .

Then she thought of Quinn again and his promise to protect her. She wanted to believe him. When he was there, right beside her, she did.

But it was the middle of the night, and her brain was hazy. She only wanted to sleep. The sheets twisted around her as she turned again and finally drifted off.

When the phone rang, she groped for it. Half dreaming, she thought it was her mother calling to scold her for being late for rehearsal. "Yes," she mumbled into the receiver. "Yes, I'm coming."

"I can't sleep. I can't sleep for thinking of you."

The whisper had a low, desperate edge to it that shocked Chantel fully awake.

"You have to stop this."

"But I can't. I've tried, but I can't. Don't you know what you do to me? Every time I see you, every time I'm near you, I —"

"No!" she shouted into the phone. Then, to her disgust, she began to weep. "Please leave me alone. Please. I don't want to hear any more."

But she could hear him as she turned her face into the pillow. She could hear him still as she fumbled to hang up the phone. Even when she had the receiver cradled, she could hear his voice echoing in her head. Chantel curled into a ball and let the tears come.

Quinn was staring out his window when the phone rang. Cursing, he dashed across the room, hoping to get to it before it awakened Chantel. But the whispering had already started. For a moment he thought he recognized something — a speech pattern, accent, or turn of phrase. He tried to focus on it, block out the words themselves and Chantel's terror. Then his mouth tightened to a grim line as he heard Chantel plead, then begin to cry. He heard her hang up, then heard a man sobbing before the connection was broken.

After slamming down the receiver, Quinn

plunged his hands into his pockets, his fingers balling into fists. He'd lost something, maybe something vital because his concentration and his objectivity had been broken when she'd begun to cry.

The woman was making him soft. He couldn't allow it. Wouldn't allow it. He had to leave her alone. She'd *want* to be alone, he told himself. She wouldn't like to have him see her now that she'd lost control. A woman like Chantel would shed her tears in private. Even if she looked for consolation, the last person she'd want it from was him. Struggling against an overpowering sense of rage and helplessness, he stalked back to the window.

She'd sounded so frightened.

He couldn't leave her alone now. Not now, he thought as he pounded his clenched hand lightly against the windowsill. She might want to be alone, but she needed to be with him. He only hoped he could figure out what to do once he was with her.

There were a few slashes of moonlight coming through her windows. They turned everything to silver. He came in quietly, hoping she'd fallen asleep again and that he could just check on her, maybe sit with her awhile without her being aware of it. If she knew how badly he wanted to be with her, protect her — damn it, cherish her — wouldn't that give her all the more reason to push him aside?

He'd never had to use caution with a woman before. Because, he was forced to admit, no woman had really mattered until her. And she mattered too much.

She wasn't asleep. Quinn could hear her muffled weeping as he crossed to the bed. He stopped where he was, terrified by the small, helpless sound. He knew how a grenade sounded when it exploded in the dirt and sent shrapnel hurtling through the air. He'd heard the horrific noise of gunfire and the unspeakable sound of a bullet striking flesh. Those were things he'd faced with more confidence than he faced Chantel's quiet sobbing with now.

If she had been angry, he could have played on it. If she had merely been frightened, he could have insulted her out of it. But she was weeping.

Soundlessly he went to the side of the bed and crouched down. Wishing he knew the right words but knowing he didn't, he laid a hand on her hair. At his touch she sprang up, screaming.

"It's me. It's only me." He took both her hands and squeezed. "Relax. No one's going to hurt you."

"Quinn." Her hand went limp in his, then tensed again as she fought for control. "You startled me."

"Sorry." The moonlight was strong enough that he could see her face, and the tears damp on her cheeks. "You okay?"

"Yes." Her chest was hurtfully tight, her throat raw from unshed tears. "Yes, I'm fine. I guess you heard the phone."

"I heard it." He dropped her hands because he was afraid he'd break her fingers. "Why don't I get you something? Water." He stuck his hands in his pockets again. "Something."

"No. I don't need anything." She brought the heels of her hands over her face to dry her tears. "I couldn't keep him talking. I just couldn't do it."

"It's all right."

"No, it's not." Bringing her knees up, she dropped her head on them. "It's my problem, and as long as I keep running from it it's not going away. Everything you've said so far has been true, everything you've done has been right, and I haven't been holding up my end."

"Nobody's blaming you, Chantel." He started to reach out for her again, to touch her creamy shoulders, which were slumped in despair. Catching himself, Quinn clenched his hand. "You should try to get some sleep."

"Yeah."

He strained against his own helplessness. Where had he gotten the stupid idea that she needed him? He didn't know the way to comfort and soothe. He didn't have the pretty words that would relax her and help her sleep again. He had nothing but a rage boiling inside him and a fierce desire to keep her safe. Neither of those would help her now.

"Look, I can get you something. Go downstairs and make, I don't know, some tea."

With her face still pressed against her knees, she squeezed her eyes tight. "No, thanks, I'll be fine."

"Damn it, I want to do something." The explosion ripped out of him before he could stop it. "I can't stand seeing you like this. Let me get you some aspirin, or sit in the chair until you can get to sleep. Something. You can't ask me to just leave you alone."

"Hold me." The words came out in a sob as she lifted her head. "Could you just hold me a minute?"

He sat beside her and, gathering her close, pressed her head to his shoulder.

"Sure. As long as you want. Go ahead and let go, angel."

She didn't have the strength to stop it, and she no longer wanted to. With his arms strong around her, she let the full force of the tears come. Quinn cradled her close and murmured things he hoped would help, things he wasn't even certain she heard. When she began to quiet, he stroked the hair back from her face and said nothing at all.

"Quinn?"

"Hmmm?"

"Thanks."

"Any time."

"I don't make a habit of it." She sniffled. "Got a handkerchief?"

"No."

Reluctant to shift away even slightly, she reached for a tissue on her bedside table. "I guess I figured a man like you would head for the hills when a woman started —" she sniffled again "— blubbering."

"This is different."

She tilted her head back. Her eyes were swollen, her cheeks tear-streaked. "Why?"

"It's just different." He brushed a tear from her lashes. Then, though he felt foolish, he let the moisture linger on his thumb. "Feel better?"

"Yes." She did, unaccountably, for she'd never believed tears solved anything. Now that they were shed she felt drained and embarrassed. "I'd, ah . . . appreciate it if we both forgot about this lapse in the morning."

"Never give yourself an inch, do you?"

"I hate to cry."

She said it with such bitter finality that he knew she'd shed hot tears over something before. Or someone. "Me too."

That made her smile. "You're a nice guy when you put a little effort into it."

"I try not to let it happen often." He stroked her hair again before he shifted her closer. It hadn't been so hard to comfort, he discovered. It wasn't so hard to be needed. "Think you can sleep now?"

"I guess." She closed her eyes, discovering it felt enormously good to let her cheek rest against his.

He ran a comforting hand over her back, then tensed when he felt silk give way to flesh. "Tomorrow's Sunday. You can stay in bed all day."

"I have a photo session at one." With her eyes still closed, she explored the muscles of his shoulders with her fingertips.

"You can cancel it."

"I'll be okay. The photographer's accommodating me because of the shooting schedule."

"Then you'd better get some rest or you'll look like hell."

"Thanks a lot."

"You're welcome."

When he drew her back, she tilted her head up and smiled at him. His fingers tensed on her shoulders, and hers on his, and her smile faded. The need vibrated between them so urgently that it set the air humming.

"I'd better go."

"No." The decision had already been made, she knew, perhaps before they'd even met. Her heart had just accepted it. She loved. There was no changing it. Until now, until him, she hadn't known how much she needed to have the chance to love again. "I want you to stay." She slid her hands over his shoulders. "I want you to make love with me."

The ache that had begun to throb just from looking at her turned sharp and stabbing — a painfully sweet sensation. Her hands felt so cool on his skin. Her eyes looked so warm and dark. The moonlight dappled over her like a dream, but he couldn't afford to forget reality.

"Chantel, I want you so much right now I

can hardly breathe. But . . ." He slid his hands up to her wrists. "I don't know if I could live with the fact that this happened between us because you were scared and shaky."

A smile curved her lips as she brought them closer to his. "Haven't you figured out yet that I know what I want?" She turned her head slightly so that her kiss brushed his chin. "Didn't you say that a man could tell just by the way a woman looked at him? Can't you see the way I'm looking at you?"

"Maybe I only see the way I want you to look." But his fingers had tangled in her hair.

"I want you to stay," she repeated, "not because I'm scared. I want you to stay because of the way you make me feel when you kiss me. When you hold me. When you touch me." She rubbed her cheek against his. "I want you to stay because you can make me forget there's anything outside of this room."

Something snapped inside him. Some would call it control. With an oath, he dragged his hands through her hair and plundered her mouth.

She was everything dark and desperate and desirable. She was pure aphrodisiac. As they knelt on the bed he let his dreams spring to life and rained kisses over her face, her hair, her throat. The scent that was so much a part of her misted through his brain like a fog. And she trembled. Not on cue but from pleasure, from the pleasure he gave her. Half-mad, he crushed his lips to hers again and tasted her passion.

Never before and, she was certain, never again, would a man bring her to life this way. Never before and never again would she want like this. Her body was like a furnace, pumping heat and energy while her mind was flooded with a brilliant kaleidoscope of sensation. No, never again would a man bring her this, because there was only one man. She'd known it, somehow, from the first.

Everything was so clear. She felt the scrape of his chin over her shoulder, felt the mattress sink under their combined weights as they knelt torso-to-torso. She could see the moonlight against his skin as she ran her hands over his shoulders and down. His muscles contracted at her touch, and she heard the soft hiss of his indrawn breath. Desperation flavored his kisses and fueled her own need. A kaleidoscope, a whirlwind, a race. The scents from her garden crept into the room. With a gurgle of delight, she lowered her lips to his shoulder and nipped.

A man could lose his mind and his soul to her. Quinn felt his chest constrict as he ran his hands freely over her. Pain and power . . . they were both twined together in his need for her. She made him hurt and made him soar just by being in his arms.

It wasn't just the perfection of form, of face, but the wild, wanton sexuality she had encased in glittering ice. Released, it was a Pandora's box of emotions, some dark, some dangerous, some desperately exciting.

He wouldn't resist her. He couldn't. He could feel her tremble, hear her moan as he touched and tasted and tempted. Her skin was hot, already damp. Her breath caught on his name. Tonight, even if it was just for tonight, he would make her as frenzied as he.

He gathered her hair in his hand, drawing her head back to expose the long white line of her throat. Her pulse beat frantically as he traced his tongue over it. Her hands moved over his chest, then lower, and his stomach muscles quivered at her touch. As she tugged at the snap on his jeans, he found her breast through the thin silk she wore. When he drew both silk and flesh into his mouth, she strained against him, shuddering. Her throat filled with indistinct murmurs of pleasure, she tugged the denim over his hips.

The feel of her hands on him drove every rational thought from his mind. In one crazed movement he ripped the silk from her, rending it down the middle. Her gasp was muffled against his mouth as he dragged her down beneath him.

He couldn't think. He could only feel. When he plunged into her she was so warm, so moist. He wondered if a man could die from being given his ultimate wish. Then she was wrapped around him, driving him even as he sought to drive her. He could see her, her hair spread out on tumbled white sheets, her eyes half closed, her lips slightly parted as the breath trembled out.

"Quinn." His name whispered from her as she was tossed by titanic waves of sensation. Heat, light, wind. Nothing had prepared her for this. She tried to tell him, but his lips were on hers again. She was a part of him. Release came in a torrent that left her too stunned for speech.

She didn't know what to say. Would he expect some clever phrase, some easy words? It wasn't possible to explain that she had given herself to only one other man and never, truly never, like this. If it hadn't mattered so much — if he hadn't mattered so much — she was sure she could have come up with something to break the long silence and the tension she felt building again.

He didn't know what to say. He'd taken her like a madman. She deserved better, more care, certainly more finesse. If only he hadn't lost control. But he had, Quinn reminded himself ruthlessly. He couldn't change that any more than he could change the fact that he'd damaged whatever might have been growing between them. He could only hope it wasn't too late to repair it.

Both of them tensed, then turned, then spoke each other's names at the same time. The awkwardness lasted only a moment before they grinned.

"I was thinking you were right," she began, "about me needing a script. I can't think of what I want to say."

"I've been having some trouble with that myself." He took her hand and brought it to his lips. "I guess I was a little rough."

"Were you?" Amused and relieved, Chantel groped for the remains of her silk teddy. Lifting a brow, she dropped it on his chest.

Quinn rubbed the material between his thumb and forefinger. "You could deduct it from my check."

"I intend to. Three hundred and fifty."

"Three hundred and fifty?" He rose on one elbow and examined the ripped silk more carefully. "You've got to be crazy to spend three-fifty on something you sleep in."

"I enjoy indulging myself." To prove her point, she leaned over and nibbled on his lips. "And under the circumstances, I think it only fair that I deduct half the price."

"Half?"

"It was a joint effort." She smiled and ran a fingertip over his chest. "Besides, it was worth it."

"Was it?" His hand came up her leg to rest on her hip. "You sure?"

"Well, I'm a cautious woman, and you know what they say in the business."

"No." Her hair teased his shoulders as she leaned over him. "What do they say in the business?"

"Take 2," Chantel sighed, lowering herself to him.

Chapter Eight

"Quinn, I promise you, this is going to take a good three hours, maybe four." Chantel got out of the car, then leaned over to take her garment bag from the hook by the passenger door.

He noticed how nicely the slim skirt fit over her bottom. "I can be patient."

"A photo session is often very tedious for the people involved, much less for someone who just has to sit there."

"Let me worry about that," he advised, and took the bag from her.

"I have to worry about it. Knowing you're hanging around, grumbling under your breath, is going to make me tense." Chantel pressed a buzzer on the outside door, then tipped down her sunglasses to peer over them. "And tension will show in the pictures. This layout for *The Scene* is very important."

He pushed the glasses back up on her nose. "So are you."

It warmed her. She no longer knew how

to pretend it didn't. Chantel rose on her toes to brush a kiss over his lips. "I appreciate that. But I'll be perfectly safe. Margot will be there to do my hair, and the makeup artist is a freelancer I've worked with before. Mrs. Alice Cooke. They have to stay for the whole session. I'll be surrounded by well-meaning women."

"And the photographer," he reminded her. "I'm not letting you alone with this Bryan Mitchell or any other man."

Chantel started to correct him, then thought better of it. A woman was entitled to take every advantage offered. She ran a finger over the collar of his shirt. "Jealous?"

"Bryan Mitchell." The voice coming through the intercom was low, smooth and feminine.

"It's Chantel O'Hurley for the one o'clock session."

"Right on time."

There was a mechanical buzz from inside the door, and then it unlatched.

"Bryan Mitchell is a tall, gorgeous blonde," Chantel began as they climbed the inside stairs. "We've been friends for years."

Quinn wrapped his fingers around hers. "All the more reason I'm not leaving you alone with him. Until this thing is settled, the only man you're having solitary dealings with is me."

"Well." Chantel paused at the studio door and wrapped her arms around him. "I like that," she murmured, and met his lips with hers.

"I bet you do." Bryan stood in the open doorway, grinning.

"Quinn Doran." Chantel laid a hand lightly on his arm. "Bryan Mitchell."

The photographer was indeed tall, blond and gorgeous. She was also a woman. Quinn shot Chantel a look as she smiled. "Nice meeting you."

Bryan offered him a hand, already wondering if she could convince him to sit for her. "Welcome to chaos," she told them as she gestured them inside. "I'm still setting up. Chantel, you know where the cold drinks are. Hairdressing and makeup are in the back room having an argument about fashion. Personally, I can't get emotionally involved over whether henna is back to stay." As she spoke, she walked over to a set of white umbrellas and adjusted them.

Chantel walked to a cramped little room off the side of the studio and poked in the refrigerator. "Quinn, it's going to be like this for hours. There must be something else you want to do."

He could hear the other two women chattering in the back room. Something about facial packs and eye tucks. "I can think of a couple dozen."

"Then go do them." Chantel set down the bottle of soda to take both of his hands. "Bryan had the security system installed a few months ago when there was a rash of robberies in the neighborhood. No one gets through the outside door unless she releases the lock. I'm surrounded by women who'll be fussing over me for hours, and you'll distract all of us. Go play some handball or something."

She was right. She'd be safe here, and he'd be in the way — as well as unmercifully bored. Then, too, it would help him to have a couple of hours away from her, a couple of hours of pure physical exertion. Would he work her out of his system?

"Gym's a couple of blocks down," he muttered.

"Jim who?"

"*The* gym," he corrected, putting his hands on her hips.

"You mean one of those places with weights and nasty machines that make you grunt and sweat?"

"More or less." Taking out his notebook, he wrote down a name and number.

"Call me when you're finished and I'll come back and pick you up."

"Rizzo's." She kept her face bland as she looked up at him. "Sounds serious."

"Just call." He leaned down to bite her lightly on the bottom lip. "Why don't you go make yourself beautiful?"

She kept her arms around him as she lifted a brow. "Aren't I already?"

He knew she hadn't so much as picked up a tube of mascara that morning. Her eyes were blue and brilliant, her skin luminous and pale. Fresh and dewy, as it was now, her beauty was heartbreaking. He lifted a hand to skim it over her cheek. "Such a hag."

Before she could retaliate he had her close, cutting off her breath in a kiss that seemed to last for hours. He needed to lift weights, Quinn thought. He had to sweat some of the need for her out of his system.

"Try to do something about that face, will you?"

"Take a walk, Doran."

He grinned at her, then slipped back into the studio. Chantel let out a shaky breath and leaned her palms against the cluttered counter beside the refrigerator. There was nothing she could do, and she was nearly ready to admit there was nothing she wanted to do, about the fact that she was in love with him. It was probably a mistake, a desperate one, but it had already been made.

Somehow, if she could somehow draw back a part of herself, she wouldn't be so devastated when he went his own way. And he would, wouldn't he? A man like Quinn lived alone, worked alone, walked alone. When his job was over he'd kiss her goodbye and go. She caught her bottom lip between her teeth and straightened. No, he wouldn't. Not if she had anything to do with it.

You're going to lose this match, Doran, she promised herself. No way was he going to walk away and leave her.

"Chantel, they're ready for you."

She was ready, too. Chantel left the drink on the counter. She was more than ready.

For two hours she worked nonstop. Her hair was frizzed, smoothed, sprayed and gelled. Her face was painted and powdered. Every time she changed her outfit her hair and face were subtly altered to enhance the look. Bryan worked with a slow, steady enthusiasm, as she always did.

"I haven't asked you how Shade is."

"Put your right hand on your left shoulder," Bryan instructed. "Spread your fingers. Good. Shade's terrific. He's home changing diapers." She caught Chantel's quick, mischievous grin on film."

"That I'd like to see."

"He's great at it. Organized, you know."

"Well, I can tell you, you don't look as though you had a baby two months ago."

"Who has time to eat? Tilt your chin up and try for aloof. That's it." She crouched, shifting angles. "Andrew Colby is a ten-pound slave driver."

"And you're crazy about him."

Bryan lowered her camera and beamed. "He's the most fantastic baby. Between Shade and me, we've taken at least five hundred rolls of film. Every day there's some little change." She tossed her long blond braid behind her back. "You can see how bright he is just by the way he looks at things. Just yesterday he —" She cut herself off with a laugh. "Stop me. It's an obsession."

"No." Chantel smiled, though the quick pang of envy she felt surprised her. "It's lovely."

"It is, you know. I never saw myself as a mother." She lifted the camera back into place. "Now I can't imagine life without Andrew. Or Shade."

"The right man can change your outlook, I guess."

Bryan decided the wistful expression that

flitted across Chantel's face would be the best shot yet. "You sure make my work easier."

Bringing herself back, Chantel looked at the camera. "How's that?"

"Turn to the side and look over your shoulder. A bit more. Smolder a little." She pressed the shutter four times in rapid succession. "A face like yours is always a pleasure to shoot, especially when you bring so much to it. But I didn't expect the bonus."

"What bonus?" Chantel asked as she shifted to look over her other shoulder.

"There's nothing more terrific than photographing a woman in love. Close your mouth," she ordered, then lowered her camera to stretch her shoulders.

Slowly Chantel turned to face Bryan again. "It's that obvious?"

"Don't you want it to be?"

"No . . . yes. I don't know." She pushed a hand through her carefully groomed hair. "I don't want to make a fool of myself."

"That kind of goes hand in hand with falling in love, but I think you'll survive it. He's got a great face. I don't suppose you could talk him into sitting for me."

"Maybe if you bound him hand and foot. Bryan, how did you handle Shade?"

Bryan took a chocolate bar out of her back

pocket. "*You're* asking *me* for advice on men?"

Chantel accepted a sliver of the chocolate. "Don't let it get around."

"Have you felt like murdering him yet?"

"Several times."

"You're making progress. The best thing I can tell you is to let things happen. We're wrapped here." She bit into the candy. "If I were you, I wouldn't waste what's left of the weekend."

The gym smelt like men. Damp, athletic men. The air was filled with sweat and swearing. Most of the patrons had stripped down to shorts, and a few had added T-shirts. On a mat, a man with weights on his legs grunted his way through a series of sit-ups. On a bench press, another man swore repetitively every time he extended the bar over his head. The equipment was top-notch, but it had long since lost its shine.

Chantel strolled in and absorbed, both brows lifted. The first one who saw her was a young man pulling weights up the walls with two ropes. He was working steadily, the veins in his neck bulging out as he rotated his arms. His mouth dropped open and the ropes snapped back against the wall. Chantel smiled at him.

Careful to keep her skirts clear, she circled around the bench press. The man stopped swearing as his eyes bugged out. It took less than ten seconds for the noisy, steamy gym to drop into silence. Then she saw Quinn.

He hadn't noticed the sudden quiet. With his back to the room, he was systematically jabbing at a punching bag. Its buffeting noise was the only sound in the room. He looked magnificent, legs spread, eyes intense, his powerful back tensed as he concentrated on his timing. The small brown bag was a blur as his fists never let it rest. Chantel walked over to him, waited a moment, then ran a fingertip down his back.

"Hello, darling."

He swore and spun, his hand still fisted and lifted. Chantel raised a brow, then her chin, as if inviting him to take his best shot.

"What the hell are you doing here?"

"Watching you." She took a finger and pushed at the bag. "Tell me, what's the purpose of beating at this little thing?"

"I told you to call me." He swiped sweat out of his eyes in order to glare at her better.

"I felt like a walk. Besides, I wanted to see where a man like you . . . played." Deliberately she looked over her shoulder and scanned the room. "Fascinating."

Every man in the room sucked in his stomach.

With an oath, Quinn took her by the arm. "You must be crazy. You don't belong in a place like this."

"Why ever not?" As they passed the man on the bench press, Chantel sent him a brilliant smile. The weights clattered against the safety bar.

"Cut that out," he muttered. "Rizzo, I'm using your office."

"Oh, where is he?" As he dragged her out, Chantel glanced back. "I'm dying to meet him."

"Shut up. Do you have to walk in here with legs like that?"

"They're all I have to walk on."

"Sit." He shoved her into a torn plastic chair. "What the hell am I supposed to do with you?"

"Would you like a multiple choice?"

"This isn't a joke, damn it." He pushed at the clutter on Rizzo's desk until he found a crumpled pack of Camels. "Look, Chantel, we made an arrangement. You were supposed to call. There are reasons." He shook out a cigarette and lit it.

"Quinn, it's a beautiful afternoon and it wasn't far. There isn't much opportunity to stroll in L.A., and I couldn't resist. If you're going to tell me I can't walk two blocks on a public street in broad daylight, I'll scream." She glanced toward the door. "I can't imagine what your, ah, associates would make of that."

He exhaled a long stream of smoke, then crushed the cigarette into a mess of brown tobacco and white paper. "You go nowhere without me. You had instructions, Chantel, and I trusted you to follow them."

"Oh, lighten up." She rose and put her palms on his bare chest.

"I'm sweating like a pig," he muttered, taking her wrists.

"I noticed. I don't know what it is that attracts men to a place that smells like old athletic socks, but if this is how you keep in shape —" she glanced down approvingly "— I might just have to install a gym at home."

"Don't change the subject."

"What subject was that?"

"I don't want anything to happen to you."

She touched her tongue to her upper lip and edged closer. "Why? You've already been paid for this week."

"I don't care about the damn money," he said with violence.

"What do you care about, Quinn?"

"You." He said it between his teeth before he spun away. He'd thought he needed space, just some space and time to get his equilibrium back. There wasn't that much space in the whole world. "Don't pull anything like this again."

"All right. I'm sorry."

"I've got to shower. Stay in here."

When the door slammed at his back, Chantel sat again. He cared. She closed her eyes and hugged the knowledge to her. He cared about her. If she'd gotten him to say it, the next step was getting him to like it.

"How long are you going to be angry?"

They were driving home with the top down. Chantel had let the first fifteen minutes pass in silence.

"I'm not angry."

"You're clenching your teeth."

"Consider yourself lucky that's all I'm doing."

"Quinn, I've already said I was sorry. I'm not going to apologize again."

"No one's asking you to." He downshifted around a curve. "What I am asking is that you take the situation you're in seriously."

"You don't think I am?"

"Not after that little stunt of yours this afternoon."

She shifted in her seat. The wind picked up her hair and tossed it as her temper snapped. "Stop treating me like a child. I understand the situation I'm in perfectly. I live with it twenty-four hours a day, every day, every night. Every time the phone rings, every time I go through my mail. When I go to sleep at night, that's what I'm thinking of. When I wake up in the morning, that's what I'm thinking of. If I can't have an hour now and then when I can push it aside, I'll go crazy. I'm trying to survive, Doran. Don't talk to me as though I'm irresponsible."

She shifted away again, and again silence reigned. He was right, Quinn told himself as he slacked his speed. But so was she. There were times, because she put up such a good front, when he believed she'd forgotten she was in any danger. She never forgot, he realized. She just refused to buckle — except in her private moments. He didn't know how to tell her he loved her for that above everything else.

Loved her. That was a tough one to swallow, but then the truth often was. The more his feelings for her grew, the more he worried about her well-being. He knew she worked hard, and for long hours. With the kind of strain she was under, she could only keep up that pace for a limited time. Even a woman as strong-willed as Chantel would lose eventually.

Damn it, he wished he had something, anything, to go on. They were moving into their third week, and he was no closer to putting things right than he had been on the first day. He needed to see her safe, secure, content. Even though he was afraid that once she was she'd write him a check and kiss him off.

Quinn's hands tightened on the wheel, then gradually relaxed. She was going to have a fight on her hands when it came to that.

Relax, he told himself. She wasn't going to get away. Moving only his eyes, he took in the stiff, angry way she sat. Angel, he told her silently, I'm just the man to clip your wings.

Quinn tossed his arm casually over the back of the seat. "You're pouting."

"Go to hell."

"You're going to get lines all over your face if you keep that up. Then where will you be?"

"Kiss my —"

"Love to." He pulled over to the side of the road. She didn't even have the chance to snarl at him before he gathered her close.

"Why don't I start with that homely face of yours and work my way down?"

"No."

"Okay, if you'd rather I take it from the bottom up."

When he started to shift her, she began to struggle in earnest. "Stop it. I don't want you to kiss me anywhere."

"Are you sure?" He brought her wrist to his lips and brushed them over the inside. "How about there?"

"No."

"Here, then." He pressed his mouth to the side of her throat. She stopped struggling.

"No."

"Well, other options are a little risky on the side of the road, but if you insist —"

"Stop." The laughter bubbled up as she shoved him away. Chantel leaned against the door and crossed her arms. "You creep."

"I love it when you insult me."

"Then you're going to love this," she began, but he was too quick. Whatever she'd had in mind was muffled against his mouth. Response came instantly, from the heart. Her arms went around him and her lips parted. For a moment there was nothing but the warm late-afternoon sun and sheer, unbridled pleasure.

Her eyes stayed closed, seconds after he'd drawn his lips from hers. When they opened, slowly, the irises were dark and clouded. "Are you trying to make up?" she murmured.

"For what?"

Her lips curved as she framed his face with her hands. "Never mind. Let's go home, Quinn."

He touched his lips to hers again, lingering, before he sat back and started the engine. "By the way, Rizzo wanted to know if he could have an autographed picture for his office."

Chantel laughed, then sat back to enjoy the rest of the drive. As they rode by the high wall surrounding her grounds, she began to toy with the idea of a long dip in the pool. Bryan was right. It would be a pity to waste what was left of the weekend. Even as she turned to ask Quinn to join her, he was bringing the car to a fast stop.

"Quinn, we really should wait until we're *inside*."

"There's a car in front of the gates." His tone had her tensing as she looked around. "A man's there, see? Looks like he's causing quite a bit of commotion."

"You don't think that —" She moistened

her lips. "He wouldn't come right to the front gate."

"Why don't we find out?" He took the keys from the ignition and unlocked the glove compartment. Chantel watched as he drew out a revolver. It was nothing like her dainty little .22. And she was just as certain it wasn't unloaded.

"Quinn."

"Stay here."

"No, I —"

"Don't argue."

"But I don't want you to . . ." As the argument at the gate heated up, the voices drifted to her. Listening intently, Chantel tightened her grip on Quinn. "I don't believe it," she murmured. She squinted, trying to make out the figure in the distance. "I just don't believe it," she repeated, and sprang out of the car before Quinn could stop her.

"Chantel!"

"It's Pop." Laughing, she spun back to Quinn. "It's Pop. My father." Her long legs flashed as she sped up the rest of the road. "Pop!" Still laughing, she threw her arms wide.

Frank O'Hurley turned from his spirited argument with the guard. His thin face erupted into a grin. "There's my girl." Spry and wiry, he pumped down the remaining distance and caught Chantel close. With a whoop, he spun her in three dizzying circles. "How's my little princess?"

"Surprised." She kissed his baby-smooth face, then hugged him again. He smelled, as he always did, of powder and peppermint. "I didn't know you were coming."

"Don't need an invitation, do I?"

"Don't be silly."

"Well, tell that to the joker on the other side of the gate. The idiot wouldn't let me in even when I told him I was your own flesh and blood."

"I'm sorry, Miss O'Hurley." The stiff-faced man behind the gate speared Frank with a look. The crazy old man had threatened to pull out his tongue and wrap it around his neck. "There was no one here to verify."

"That's all right."

"All right?" Frank piped up. He was primed and ready for a donnybrook. "All right when your own father's treated like a trespasser?"

"Don't be cranky." Chantel brushed at his lapels. "I've added to the security, that's all."

"Why?" Immediately alert, he cupped Chantel's chin. "What's wrong?"

"It's nothing. We'll get into all that later. Now I'm just glad to see you." She glanced back at the dusty rental car. "Where's Mom?"

"Said she wasn't fit to see anyone until she'd been to the beauty parlor. I wasn't going to sit around cooling my heels while she's getting primped up. She'll be taking a cab out later."

"But tell me what you're doing here, how long you can stay. What —"

"God be praised, girl, can't it wait until a man's washed the dust out of his throat? Drove clear from Vegas today."

"Vegas? I didn't know you had a gig in Vegas."

"You don't know everything." He tweaked her nose, then looked over her shoulder as Quinn pulled up. "Now who might this be?"

"That's Quinn." She shot him a quick look. "Quinn Doran. You're right, Pop, we can talk better inside — especially after you've had a glass of the Irish."

"Now you're talking." Frank hopped back in his car, then sailed through the now-open gates. Chantel saw him look down his nose at the guard.

"Your father?" Quinn asked when she climbed back in the car.

"Yes, I wasn't expecting him, but that's nothing new." Her fingers twisted together. "You put the gun away?"

He lifted a hand to the guard as he drove through. "Don't worry."

"But I am. I didn't want to bring my family into all this." Chantel pressed the bridge of her nose between her thumb and forefinger. "I'm going to have to tell them something. He's seen the guard at the gates. He's bound to notice the men patrolling the grounds."

"Why don't you try the truth?"

"I don't want to worry my parents. Damn, I only get to see them three or four times a year, and now this." She looked at Quinn as he slowed at the end of the drive. "And I have to explain you."

"The truth," he repeated.

"All right. I can't think of anything else." She put a hand on his arm before he could climb out. "But I'll do it my way. I want to play it down as much as possible."

"Well now." Beaming and affable, Frank strolled over to the car. "Looks like you've got yourself a fine strong fellow here, Chantel."

"Quinn Doran, my father, Frank O'Hurley."

"Pleased to meet you." Frank offered a

218

hand and pumped Quinn's exuberantly. "Wouldn't mind helping me in with the bags, would you, son?"

Chantel had to smile when Frank popped open his trunk and took out a small shoulder bag, leaving two large cases for Quinn. "You never change," she murmured hooking an arm through his to lead him into the house.

"Just leave them there," she told Quinn, gesturing to the base of the staircase. "You can take them up later."

"Thanks."

She met his sarcasm with an easy smile. "Why don't you two go into the living room and have a drink? I want to tell the cook there'll be two more for dinner." Leaving Quinn with a brief warning look, she started down the hall.

"Well, son, I don't know about you," Frank said, giving Quinn a solid slap on the back. "But I could use a drink." He trotted off into the living room and headed directly to the bar. "What's your pleasure?"

"Scotch."

Frank shrugged his narrow shoulders, then poured. "To each his own." Locating the bottle of whiskey, he gave a satisfied grunt and poured a generous three fingers. "Well, now . . . Quinn, is it? Why don't we drink to my girl?" He tapped his glass solidly against Quinn's without regard for the pricey Rosenthal crystal, then swallowed deeply. "Now that's a drink a man can wrap his heart around. Have a seat, son, have a seat." Still playing the congenial host, he gestured to a chair before finding one for himself. "Now . . ." He settled back and sighed. Then, abruptly, his eyes were shrewd and sharp. "Just what are you doing with my daughter?"

"Pop." Grateful for her timing, Chantel strolled into the room, then sat on the arm of her father's chair. "You'll have to excuse him, Quinn. He's never been subtle."

Quinn regarded his Scotch for a moment. "Seems like a reasonable question to me."

"There." Satisfied with what he saw, Frank nodded. "We're going to get along just fine."

"I wouldn't be surprised," she murmured ruffling her father's hair. "So tell me how it went in Vegas."

"Be glad to." He sipped his whiskey again, appreciating its smooth heat. "Just as soon as you explain why you have a trained gorilla at your front gate."

"I told you, I added some security." But when she started to rise, Frank put a firm hand on her knee.

"You wouldn't try to con an old hand like me, would you, princess?"

It would be useless, she admitted, and settled back. "I've been getting some annoying phone calls, that's all. It seemed wise to take a few precautions."

"What kind of phone calls?"

"Just nuisance calls."

"Chantel." He knew his daughter too well. A few nuisance calls would have been brushed off, laughed off and forgotten. "Is someone threatening you?"

"No. No, it's nothing like that." Realizing she was being backed into a corner, she shot a pleading look at Quinn.

"I still opt for the truth," he said simply.

"Thanks for the help."

"Just be quiet," Frank told her, and there was such uncharacteristic authority in his tone that she closed her mouth instantly. "You tell me what's going on," he ordered Quinn. "And what you have to do with it."

"Quinn —"

"Chantel Margaret Louise O'Hurley, shut your mouth and keep it shut."

When she did, Quinn could only smile. "Nice trick," he said to Frank.

"I use it selectively to keep it fresh." Frank swallowed the rest of his whiskey. "Let's hear it."

Briefly, concisely, Quinn outlined what Chantel was dealing with. As he spoke, Frank's brows lowered, his thin face reddened and the hand still resting on Chantel's knee clenched.

"Slimy bastard." Frank rose out of the chair like a terrier ready to charge. "If you're a detective, Quinn Doran, why in hell haven't you found him?"

"Because he hasn't made a mistake." Quinn set down his glass and met Frank's outraged glare levelly. "But he will, and I'll find him."

"If he hurts my girl —"

"He's not going to get near her," Quinn interrupted flatly. "Because he has to go through me first."

Frank swallowed his fury — it was something he didn't often bother to do — and measured the man in front of him. He'd always prided himself on being a good judge of character. You needed to know whether to raise your fists or laugh and back off. The man in front of him was hard as a rock and mean as they came. If he had to trust his daughter to someone, this was the one.

"So. You're staying here, in the house, with Chantel."

"That's right. I'm going to take care of

her, Mr. O'Hurley. You have my word on that."

Frank hesitated only a moment before his teeth showed in a smile. "If you don't, I'll skin you alive. And make it Frank."

Cool and regal, Chantel rose. "Perhaps I could say a word now."

"Don't put that face on with me, girl." Frank crossed to her, then gently framed her face in his hands. "You should have come to your family with this."

"There was no point in worrying you."

"Point?" Frank shook his head from side to side. "We're family. We're the O'Hurleys. We stick together."

"Pop, Maddy's getting married at the end of the week. Abby's pregnant. Trace is —"

"You'll kindly leave him out of it," Frank said stiffly. "Family business has nothing to do with your brother. That's his choice."

"Really, Pop, after all this time you should —"

"And don't change the subject. Your mother and me, and your sisters, are entitled to worry about you."

It wasn't the time to go to her brother's defense. And Chantel wasn't entirely sure he'd care one way or the other. Now she wanted to smooth those lines of worry from her father's face.

"All right, then." She kissed him soundly. "Worry all you want, but everything that can be done is being done."

He kept his hand on her shoulder but turned to Quinn. "We're off to New York on Friday to see my daughter married off. You'll be going with us?"

"I didn't think it was necessary to drag Quinn to —"

"I'm going," he interrupted. His eyes met Chantel's in something like a challenge. "I've already made the arrangements."

"You never mentioned it to me."

"Why should I?" he countered for the simple pleasure of watching fury rise in her eyes.

"It hardly seems I'm necessary, does it?" Feeling squeezed from all sides, she bristled. "If you'll both excuse me, I'm going to go soak my head."

"Nasty little number, isn't she?" Frank asked with obvious pride as she stalked out.

"All that and more."

"It's the Irish, you know. We're either poets or fighters. O'Hurleys are a bit of both."

"I'm looking forward to meeting the rest of your family."

And they'll want to get a look at you, Frank said to himself. "Tell me, Quinn," he began in an amiable tone. "Do you intend to, ah, keep your eye on Chantel, so to speak, after this business is settled?"

Quinn studied the man across from him. It seemed it was still time for truths. "Yes. Whether she likes it or not."

Frank gave a quick laugh. "Let's have another drink."

Chapter Nine

"Mom, there's no reason for you to do that."

Molly O'Hurley carefully folded a white silk jacket in tissue. "Why should you call a maid up here?" Years of experience had Molly packing Chantel's clothes with a minimum of fuss.

"It's her job."

Molly brushed her objections away with the back of her hand. "I never feel I can speak my mind in front of maids and butlers."

Chantel looked at the suitcase and at her stacks of clothes. She'd spent the first twenty years of her life packing and unpacking. As a matter of principle, she hadn't done so in years. But she'd never been able to win a fight with her mother. Resigned, Chantel began a careful selection of her toiletries.

"I'm sorry we haven't had much time together the past few days."

"Don't be silly." Brisk and practical, Molly rattled more tissue paper. "You're in the middle of that film. Your father and I didn't expect to be entertained."

"Pop seemed to be entertained the day you came to the set."

Chuckling, Molly glanced up. She was a pretty, trim woman who managed to look a decade younger than her years with a minimum of effort. Looking at her, Chantel acknowledged that the rush and craziness of her parents' life-style suited Molly just as much as it did Frank. "He did, didn't he? Still, I don't think he should have argued with the director about how to set the scene."

"Mary has a — a sense of humor."

"Good thing." For the next few moments, they packed in silence. "Chantel, we're worried about you."

"Mom, that's exactly what I don't want you to do."

"We love you. You can't expect us to love you and not be concerned."

"I know." She slipped a bottle of perfume into a padded travel box. "That's why I didn't want to tell you about what was going on. You had to worry enough about me when I was growing up."

"You don't expect a parent to turn off the juice just because a child's past the age of twenty-one?"

"No, I suppose not." She smiled and slipped her set of makeup brushes into their cases. "But it seems like you should have less to worry about after a certain age."

"I can only tell you that one day you'll find out differently yourself."

There was that pang again. Chantel's brows drew together as she tried to ignore it. "I don't know about that," she murmured. "I *do* know I don't want this business to affect the family."

"What affects one of us affects all of us. That's that." Molly said it so matter-of-factly, Chantel was forced to smile.

"Your Irish is showing."

"And why shouldn't it?" Molly wanted to know. "Your father and I think we should come back with you after the wedding."

"Back here?" Chantel stopped to stare. "You can't. You have a gig in New Hampshire."

Molly folded a pair of linen slacks by the pleats and said with a little smile, "Chantel, your father and I have been performing for over thirty-five years. I don't think canceling one engagement is going to make much of a ripple."

"No." Chantel set down the bottles and pots in her hands to reach for her mother. "I can't tell you how much it means to know that you would. But what could you do?"

"We could be with you."

"You could hardly even do that. Mom, I'll be filming for weeks more. You've seen in the last few days how little I'm home. I'd be a wreck thinking about you sitting around here twiddling your thumbs when you'd want to be working."

"Sitting around here, as in lounging by the pool?"

Chantel's lips curved, but she shook her head. "If I could believe you'd be content for more than forty-eight hours, it would be different. Be logical, Mom. If you stayed I'd be worried because you were worried. Pop would drive the staff crazy, and I wouldn't even be around to enjoy it."

"I told Frank you'd feel this way." With a sigh, Molly touched Chantel's hair. "I always worried about you the most, you know."

"I guess I gave you the most cause."

"You did what you had to. And Trace also was going to go his own way, no matter what. Your father refused to see it, but it was there from the time he could walk. Somehow I always knew Abby and Maddy would be all right, even when Abby was going through the mess of her first marriage and Maddy was struggling to keep herself in dancing shoes. But you . . ." Molly caressed her daughter's cheek. "I was always afraid you'd miss what was beside you because you were always looking so far ahead. I want you to be happy, Chantel."

"I am. No, I am, really. These past few weeks, even with this other business hanging over my head, I've found something."

"Quinn."

Chantel made a restless movement before walking to the windows. "It's obvious to everyone but him the way I feel."

Molly had formed her own opinion of Quinn Doran. He wasn't an easy man, nor would he often be a gentle one, but her daughter didn't need an easy, gentle man. She needed one who'd give her a run for her money.

"Men are more thickheaded," Molly commented. She was a woman who knew well just how thickheaded men could be. "Why don't you tell him?"

"No." She turned back, then rested the heels of her hands on the windowsill. "At least not yet. This is going to sound foolish, but I want . . . I need him to respect me. Me," she repeated. "For what I am. I need to be certain he's not just passing the time."

"Chantel, you can't use Dustin Price as a yardstick."

"I'm not." Anger crept into her voice. She managed to control it only because her mother's eyes remained so steady. "No, I'm not. But it isn't something that's easy to forget."

"No, it's impossible. But you can't live your life with that as the foundation. Have you told Quinn about him?"

"No, I can't. Mom, there are so many complications now, why bring up another? It's been nearly seven years."

"Do you trust Quinn?"

"Yes."

"Don't you think he'd understand?"

She pressed her fingers to her eyes for a moment. "If I was sure he loved me, really sure that what's between us is real, I could tell him anything. Even that."

"I wish I could tell you there were guarantees, but I can't." Molly crossed to her and gathered Chantel close. "I can tell you that I wouldn't consider leaving you, not for a minute until everything was resolved, if I wasn't sure Quinn was going to protect you."

"He makes me feel safe. Until I met him, I didn't know anyone could." She squeezed her eyes shut. "I didn't know I needed anyone who could."

"We all need to feel safe, Chantel. And loved." Molly stroked her hair, the light silver-blond locks she'd brushed and braided so often in the past. "There's something I haven't told you. Something I should have told you a long time ago." She embraced Chantel. "I'm very proud of you."

"Oh, Mom." As the tears welled up, Molly shook her head.

"Now, none of that," she murmured. "If we go downstairs with puffy eyes, your father will be pinching at me to find out why we've been sitting up here crying." She kissed Chantel's cheek and held on for another moment. "Let's finish packing."

"Mom."

"Yes, dear."

"I've always been proud of you, too."

"Well." Molly cleared her throat, but her voice was still husky when she spoke. "That's quite a thing to hear from a grown daughter. You're going to be all right?"

"I'm going to be fine. I'm going to be terrific."

"That's my girl. Now let's be about our business." Turning away, Molly made herself busy. "Look at this." Clucking her tongue, she held up a brief nightgown fashioned of black silk and lace. "It looks like sin."

Chantel rubbed a knuckle under her eyes to dry them and giggled. "I can't give it an evaluation yet. I just bought it."

Molly held it up to the sunlight. "I think it speaks for itself."

"You like it." Pleased, Chantel came over, folded it carefully and handed it back to her mother. "A souvenir from Beverly Hills."

"Don't be silly." But Molly couldn't resist rubbing a thumb over the silk. "I couldn't wear a thing like this."

"Why not?"

"I'm the mother of four grown children."

"You didn't pick us from under cabbage leaves."

"Well, your father would . . ." She trailed off, speculating. Chantel watched a wicked gleam come into her eyes. "Thank you, dear." Molly set the nightgown apart from the rest of Chantel's lingerie. "And I'll thank you from your father in advance."

By the time they went downstairs again, Frank could be heard picking his banjo.

"He's practicing," Molly said, "so he can play at the reception. They'll have to knock him unconscious to keep him from performing."

"You know Maddy wouldn't have it any other way."

"It's about time, woman." Frank looked up as his family walked in, but his fingers never stilled. "A man needs some backup, you know. This one here —" he jerked his head toward Quinn "— won't sing a note."

"Just doing you a favor," Quinn said easily as he lounged back on the sofa.

"Never heard of a body that wouldn't sing," Frank commented. "Heard plenty that couldn't, but never one who wouldn't. Sit here, Molly, my love. Let's show the man what the O'Hurleys are made of."

Obligingly Molly sat beside him, picked up the count and launched into the song with a strong, practiced voice. Chantel sat on the arm of the sofa beside Quinn and listened to the familiar sound of her parents working together. It was good, it was solid. The tension of the past weeks drained away.

"Come on, princess, you remember the chorus."

Chantel joined in, the words and rhythm of the bright novelty number coming easily. She rarely sang on her own. To Chantel, singing was a family affair. Even now, as she added her voice to her parents', she thought of Trace and her sisters and the countless times they'd all sung that same old song.

She'd surprised him. Quinn sat back, enjoying himself, as Frank merged one tune into another. Chantel wasn't the cool movie star now, nor was she the restless, passionate woman he'd discovered beneath that facade. She was at home with the nonsense songs her father played. She was a daughter, a loving one. The innocence he'd once sensed in her was apparent as she laughed and accused her father of missing a note.

Her scent was there, dark and sultry, in contrast to her relaxed, playful behavior. He'd never seen her like this. Never known she could be like this. He wondered if she realized how much her family meant to her, if she knew how her Hollywood image faded when she was with them.

It had been a good week. Chantel didn't know of the letters that had come, because he'd intercepted them. Nor did she know that they had traced one of the calls to a phone booth downtown. Quinn saw no reason to tell her or to hit her with the fact that two of the letters had begged for a meeting in New York.

He knew her plans.

Quinn lifted a hand and ran it down her

arm. Chantel's fingers linked naturally with his. There was no point in telling her. She wouldn't be alone in New York, not for a moment. He'd already arranged for three of his best men to fly to Manhattan. Every step Chantel took would be monitored.

Frank interrupted Quinn's train of thought as he shot a challenging look at his daughter. "Do you still play that thing? Or do you use it as a doorstop?"

Chantel glanced at the white baby grand, then examined her nails. "I manage to hit a few keys."

"With a big, beautiful instrument like that you should be able to do a lot more."

"I don't want to show you up, Pop."

"That'll be the day."

With a shrug, she stood and moved to the piano. Deliberately she fluttered her lashes, sat, then went into a long, complicated arpeggio.

"You've been practicing," Frank accused, then cackled with delight.

Chantel shot a look at Quinn. "I don't spend my evenings darning socks."

Quinn acknowledged the hit with a slight inclination of his head. "Your daughter's full of surprises, Frank."

"No need to tell me that. The stories I could tell you. Why, there was the time —"

236

"Requests?" Chantel interrupted sweetly. "Unless Pop wants me to tie his tongue in a nice, neat bow."

Always cautious, Frank cleared his throat. "Why don't you do that little number your mother wouldn't let you sing until you turned eighteen?"

"Abby always did that one best."

"True enough." Frank's grin was crooked and amiable. "But you weren't half-bad." Molly managed to hide a smile as Chantel's eyes narrowed.

"Half-bad?" She wrinkled her nose at him as she gave herself a flowing introduction.

The low, torchy ballad prickled along Quinn's skin. Her voice was as smooth as the Scotch in his hand, and just as potent. The words were plaintive, vulnerable, but with her voice they became seductive. She wore white as she sat behind the glossy white piano. But he no longer thought of angels. The room grew warmer just from the sound of her voice. It seemed to weigh on him, pressing down until he was no longer sure he was even breathing.

Then she brought her gaze up from the keys to meet his.

It wasn't a song of love, but of love lost. The thought came to him then that if he lost her there were no words written that could describe his desperation. She'd made him ache before. And she'd made him burn. Now, for the first time, she made him weak.

She played the last chords with her eyes still locked on his.

"Not half-bad," Frank repeated, pleased with her delivery. "Now if you'd —"

"It's late, Frank." Molly patted his hand, loving him for the knucklehead he was. "We should go up to bed. Tomorrow's going to be a long day."

"Late? Nonsense, it's barely —"

"Late," Molly repeated. "And getting later by the minute. I have a surprise for you upstairs."

"But I was just getting — A surprise?"

"That's right. Come along, Frank. Good night, Quinn."

"Molly." But he couldn't take his eyes off Chantel.

"All right, all right, I'm coming. Good night, you two. Chantel, see if that cook of yours can make waffles in the morning, will you?"

"Night, Pop." She tilted her cheek for his kiss, but her eyes stayed locked on Quinn's.

As he climbed the stairs with his wife, Frank could be heard demanding what his surprise was.

"You were right," Quinn murmured

when the room was silent again.

"About what?"

"You are terrific." He rose and came to her. Taking both her hands, he turned them palm up and pressed his lips to the center of each one. "The more I'm with you," he murmured, "the more I know you, the more I want."

With her hands still in his, she stood. Light glowed in her eyes. "I've never in my life felt about anyone the way I feel about you. I need you to believe that."

"And I need to believe it." They were close, very close, to taking that final step. Commitments, promises, dependence. He felt himself teeter on the edge, ready, but was afraid she would pull back and away if he pressed too soon. "Tell me what you want, Chantel."

"You." She could give that answer truthfully enough without demanding more than she thought he was ready to give. "I only want to be with you."

For how long? he wanted to ask, but fear stopped him. He would take today, tonight, and fight for tomorrow. "Come to bed."

Hands linked, hearts lost, they climbed the stairs.

They left a low light burning beside the bed. Odd, she thought, that her pulse should be hammering so hard, that her nerves should be fluttering so wildly when she already knew what they could bring to each other. Why should it feel so different this time? So special. So much, she realized dimly, like the first time. The only time.

She offered her mouth, anticipating the hard demand of his.

He was gentle. He was . . . tender. As he brushed his lips lightly over hers she felt her muscles go lax and her bones melt. He cupped her face with his hands so that his thumbs traced like whispers, like promises, over her throat. She sighed his name as she felt herself float.

What kind of passion was this that crept in so quietly? Desire was there, already thrumming, but with each caress he soothed it — and stoked it. His mouth was patient, gliding over her face as if he wanted to memorize the essence of her through touch and taste. He strung small, feathery kisses down her cheekbones, then sought her mouth. His tongue traced the outline, then lingered to stroke lazily over her bottom lip. The room began to whirl inside her head.

She was priceless. This time, he promised himself, he would show her. She had a beauty he knew now reached beneath the skin. He would cherish it. He combed his fingers through her hair, delighting in the silken feel of it. He murmured, and she sighed and pressed herself against him.

As his mouth continued to explore, he began to undo the row of buttons at her back. When the material parted, he ran his hands along her spine, gently, as a man touches fragile glass. As the silk slithered to the floor, she trembled. She was warm and naked beneath it. His heart hammered in his throat. It was as though she had waited all evening for this moment with him.

Quinn drew her away to look at her, all of her, in the lamplight. She was so small, so delicate, with skin like porcelain and a form that might have been carved from alabaster. Her hair tumbled over her shoulders, ending just before the curve of her breasts. Her rib cage was narrow. He ran his hands down it, amazed that the strength he knew she possessed came from such delicacy. Her waist tapered so that he could almost span it with his hands before flaring out gently to slender hips and long, slim thighs.

"You're so beautiful." His voice was strained as he brought his gaze back to hers. "You take my breath away."

She stepped forward into his arms.

The material of his shirt was rough against her bare skin. With her eyes half closed, Chantel moved against him, urging his mouth to take its fill. Her tongue found his and began a silent, exotic seduction. All the while, his fingertips played over her as exquisitely as hers had played over the piano keys.

Through the window the breeze stirred, threatening rain. Chantel inhaled the fragrances of the night as they tangled with the musky scent of passion. Slowly, and with as much care as he had shown her, she undressed Quinn.

She rubbed her palms over the hard, coiled muscles of his shoulders, delighting in the feel. Temptingly she pressed her lips to his chest. There was a power and discipline in his body that urged her to touch, to tease. The ridges of muscles in his torso fascinated her. With a murmur of approval, she bought her lips back to his.

They lowered themselves onto the bed.

No hurry. No rush. The moment was drawn out, dreamlike, as they pleasured each other. Chantel shifted to look down at him. How could she tell him what he'd come to mean to her? How could she explain how much she needed him to be with her — now, tomorrow, forever? Did a man like Quinn believe in forever? She shook her head quickly, thrusting the questions aside.

She couldn't tell him, she couldn't ask him. But she could show him.

Softly Chantel brought her mouth to his, then ran her fingertip over it as if to test the warmth she'd elicited. Approving, she brought her lips to his again, to savor.

He hadn't known it could be like this. Even in the wildest rages of passion they'd incited in each other, he hadn't known there could be such wonder. He'd told himself before that she belonged to him, but now, with her pliant and soft in his arms, he could finally believe it. And what was more, he was hers. Completely, utterly. Love fueled by tenderness was more consuming than any madness.

He slipped into her easily, naturally. With a sigh, she accepted him. They rose together in a harmony of movement that was its own kind of beauty.

When there was nothing left to give, they gathered each other close and slept.

"Don't rush me, don't rush me." With a spring in his step, Frank waltzed in front of the skycap desk. "I'm going to make sure they don't send my banjo to Duluth."

"La Guardia." With a grin, the skycap showed Frank the stubs. "Don't worry about a thing."

"Easy for you to say. I've had that banjo longer than I've had my wife." Then, with a chuckle, he squeezed Molly's shoulder. "Not that you mean less to me, my love."

"But we run neck and neck. Did you take your Dramamine, Frank?"

"Yes, yes, don't fuss."

"Frank's a hideous air traveler," Molly put in as she pocketed the tickets and boarding passes. "That's where Chantel got it from."

Surprised, Quinn stopped in the act of hefting his small carry-on bag. "You don't like to fly?"

"I'm fine." She'd already downed half a roll of antacids and two air sickness pills.

Molly glanced at the watch on her wrist. "We'd better get moving."

"Women. Always rushing." Frank gave Quinn a slap on the back. "Why do we put up with it, boy?"

"Only game in town."

"Right you are." Delighted with the world in general, Frank cackled as he strolled through the automatic doors.

"You're feeling chipper this morning," Chantel commented dryly, refusing to acknowledge the leaden feeling in her own stomach.

"And why not?" Frank beamed as they

rode up the escalator toward their gate. "A good night's sleep's just the ticket." He quirked his brow at Molly and wondered if she'd wear that little black number again anytime soon.

As they passed through gate security, Chantel began the slow and even breathing technique that helped her get on board.

"Angel." Quinn drew her off to the side. "Don't you have a tranquilizer or something?"

"I don't take them." She twisted the strap of her bag in her fingers. "Besides, I'm fine."

He unclenched her fingers and soothed them with his. "Your hands are like ice."

"It's chilly in here."

Quinn noted a man mopping his brow as the room filled with body heat. "I didn't realize you were nervous about flying."

"Don't be silly, I fly all the time."

"I know. It must be rough."

Disgusted with herself, she stared over his shoulder. "Everyone's entitled to a phobia."

"That's right." He brought her hand to his lips. "Let me help."

She started to draw her hand away but found it held firmly. "Quinn, I feel like an idiot. I'd rather you just let it go."

"Fine. But you wouldn't mind holding

my hand during the flight, would you?"

"It's six hours," she muttered. "Six incredibly long hours."

He tilted her face to his. "We ought to be able to think of something to pass the time." As he lowered his mouth to hers, neither of them noticed a man wearing dark glasses slip into a seat in the corner of the departure lounge. Neither of them noticed the way his hands clenched into fists as he watched them.

"If we do what you're thinking of, we'll be arrested," Chantel murmured, but the tension in her shoulders eased.

Quinn nipped at her lip. "I'm surprised at you. I was thinking of gin rummy."

"Like hell." When their flight was called, she drew a deep breath and kept her hand in his. "A dollar a point?"

"You're on."

Laughing, she walked with Quinn and her parents through the gate.

The man in dark glasses rose and pulled a low-brimmed hat over his head, then took out his boarding pass. He merged with the crowd that surged onto the plane.

Chapter Ten

"Are you sure you don't mind being drafted into the family?" Chantel carefully zipped a dress into her garment bag. She'd hired one of Hollywood's leading designers to create it, but it wasn't for the stage or the screen. It wasn't every day she was maid of honor at her sister's wedding.

"Is that what you call it?" Amused, Quinn sat on the unmade bed, dressed only in a towel. There was a freshly pressed suit in the closet that he didn't even want to think about.

"I don't know what else." Preoccupied, Chantel checked her makeup bag. If she'd forgotten anything, Maddy was sure to have it — probably still in the box. "Pop said you had to be at Reed's suite an hour before the ceremony." She paused and glanced back at him. "Just what is it men do before a wedding?"

"State secret, and no, I don't mind."

She stopped again, tapping a brush against her palm. "What did you think of

Reed, Quinn? I know we only had a few hours together last night, but you must have formed an impression."

"Worried about your sister?"

"It goes with the territory."

He settled back against the pillows and looked at her. Trim slacks, a silk blouse, silver-blond hair pulled back from an extraordinary face with hammered gold combs. Chantel O'Hurley didn't look anything like a mother hen, but he'd learned to see farther than skin deep. When it came to her family, she was a marshmallow.

"Dependable, certainly successful. Meticulous, I'd guess. Conservative."

"And Maddy?"

"Scattered, theatrical and a shade wide-eyed."

"That's Maddy," Chantel murmured. "It doesn't seem as though they'd have enough in common for more than a ten-minute conversation. But —"

"But?"

"It feels right." With a sigh, she dropped the brush into her bag. "It just feels right."

"Then what are you worried about?"

"She's my baby sister."

"By how many minutes?" he asked dryly.

"Time has nothing to do with it." She said it with such offhand certainty that he was sure the question had been put to her before. "She *is* my baby sister, and she's always been the most trusting one, the most loving one. Abby's so . . . solid," she said. "And I've got enough meanness in me to keep my head above water, but Maddy . . . Maddy's the kind of woman who believes the check *is* in the mail, the alarm didn't go off or the gas gauge was broken."

"I think your sister knows exactly what she wants and how to make it work."

"So do I, really. I guess I'm just being sentimental."

Quinn arched a brow. "Why don't you come over here and be sentimental?"

She sent him a slow smile. "I thought you were waiting for room service."

"Hate to wait alone."

"Quinn, if I get back in that bed . . ."

"Yeah?"

"I'm going to make incredible love to you."

"Threats, huh?" He lay back and crossed his arms behind his head. "Why don't you come over here and say that?"

She tossed her cosmetic bag aside and walked to him. "You haven't got a chance."

"Big talk."

"I can do more than talk," she murmured, and ran her fingertips up his leg to where the towel skimmed the top of his thigh. "Much more."

Before she could prove it, Quinn grabbed her wrist and yanked so that she tumbled across his chest. Her laughter came first, then was muffled to a sigh against his lips.

It didn't seem possible that she could want him as much as she had the night before, when they'd first slipped between the linen hotel sheets, but the excitement was just as new now, just as vital.

The scent of his shower was on him, fresh and tangy. His hair was slightly damp as it brushed across her face. His body was there for her, strong, virile, unclothed. With another laugh, she pressed her lips to his throat.

"Something funny?"

"I feel safe." She tossed back her head to smile at him. "So wonderfully safe."

He brushed the hair away from her face, holding it a moment, then letting it stream through his hands. How had she come to mean so much to him in so short a time?

"Safe's not the only thing I want you to feel."

"No?" She lowered her lips to his shoulder and let her tongue glide across his skin. "What else?"

Love, loyalty, devotion. It was frightening

that those were his first thoughts. To protect himself, and maybe to protect her, he
didn't tell her that. The physical loving
wouldn't hurt either of them — not the way
emotions could.

"Why don't I show you?" In one quick
move he had Chantel on her back beneath
him. The towel around his waist was held in
place only by the press of their bodies. When
his lips found hers, she began to tug the
towel aside. Aroused, he laughed and made
quick work of the buttons on her blouse. A
knock on the door of the adjoining parlor
had them both groaning. Chantel rose on her
elbow and tossed her mussed hair back.

"You had to have breakfast, didn't you?"

"Let him bring it back later." Quinn
slipped a hand under her skirt to explore her
thigh. The knock came again, more insis-
tently this time.

"I'll get it." Shifting away from Quinn,
she adjusted her blouse. Then, with a grin,
she picked up the towel and tossed it across
the room. "You stay here." She kissed him
again, quickly. "Right here."

"You're the boss."

"Keep that in mind." Chantel was smiling
as she hurried into the parlor. Quinn would
have his breakfast, but he was going to eat it
cold.

In bed, Quinn reached over and idly turned on the radio. A little music, he thought. With the drapes still drawn, the room was dim. They might be anywhere. For a moment he let himself imagine they were in their bedroom — not in her house, not in his, not in some plush hotel, but in a home they'd made between them. When you loved, he realized, you didn't just think of now, but of always.

Maybe it was time to tell her, time to admit to her, not just to himself, that he loved her and wanted to share his life with her. His life — that meant past, present, future, not just the fleeting urge to satisfy passion, to quench desire. There was passion, but it would never be satisfied. Desire would never be quenched. And more, much more, there was emotion that swelled and expanded every moment he was with her.

He wanted her for his wife. That should have terrified him, but it almost amused him. He wanted her in all the traditional ways, the ways he'd always shrugged aside as restrictive and unimportant. A home, a family, his ring on her finger and hers on his. Quinn Doran, family man. It suddenly seemed to fit.

She might balk. She probably would.

He'd just have to apply the right kind of pressure. Thinking of it made him smile a little. Persuading Chantel O'Hurley to marry him might just be the toughest nut he'd ever cracked.

"Quinn."

"Yeah?"

"Would you come out here a minute?"

He heard it in her voice, just a hint of tension. Quinn pushed aside his fantasies and reached for his robe. He saw the flowers as soon as he stepped into the parlor. A dozen blood-red roses with their petals just opened sat on the table by the door. Chantel stood beside them, her face as white as the card she held in her hand.

"He knows I'm here." She managed to keep her voice even, almost calm. "He says he'd follow me anywhere." Her fingers were steady as she handed the card to Quinn, but when his brushed over them, he found them cold. "He says he's waiting for the perfect time."

Quinn took the note and glanced briefly at the message. In the corner of the envelope was the printed name of the florist's shop. "He's made his first mistake," he murmured. "Who brought these up?"

"A bellboy." She stared at the far wall, at a Monet print, and wondered why she felt nothing, nothing at all. "I didn't even tip him."

"Stop it."

His voice snapped her back. After one long shudder, Chantel looked at him. She wouldn't get sympathy from Quinn, or soothing words or empty promises. She didn't want them. She wanted the truth. "He's here, isn't he? He might even be in this hotel."

"Sit down." He started to take her arm, but she backed away.

"I don't need to sit down. I need some answers."

"Chantel —"

At the next knock, she pressed a hand to her mouth to muffle a scream. Swearing, Quinn pushed her into a chair then went to the door. Through the peephole he saw a room-service waiter with a breakfast tray. "It's all right," he tossed over his shoulder. "Just room service."

Quinn opened the door to let the waiter roll the cart to the table by the window. After scrawling his name on the tab, he followed the waiter to the door to take a quick scan of the hall.

"You could use some coffee," Quinn said, moving past Chantel to the breakfast tray.

"No, answers." Though her knees were

wobbly, she rose. "I'm not sure why, but I think you have them. You knew he'd be here."

Despite her refusal, Quinn poured two cups. "Yeah."

"Yeah." A dry laugh came from nowhere as she pressed her fingers to her temple. "You're not a man to elaborate, are you, Quinn? How did you know he'd be here? Sixth sense, gut hunch, instinct?"

"Any of those would do." He felt a sick curling in his stomach as he turned to face her again. "I expect him to go where you go, but in addition to that he said he'd be here in the last few notes he sent."

She crossed her arms over her chest. The chill had sprung to her skin quickly. She was beginning to feel now, and feel sharply. "You didn't think I should know?"

"If I'd thought you should know I'd have told you. Why don't you eat something?"

Yes, there were feelings now. They were boiling inside her, threatening to bubble out with the first word she spoke. Chantel walked to the table and, keeping her eyes on Quinn's, picked up a plate and very deliberately dropped it on the floor.

"Just who the hell do you think you are?" Her voice carried more venom when it was low and steady. "How dare you treat me as though I'm some brainless, gutless female who needs to be led around by the nose? I had a right to know he intended to follow me, that things would be the same here as they were on the Coast."

He could let his temper go or he could control it. Quinn sat down and picked up his coffee. Anger had taken the dazed look out of her eyes. He'd let her take it as far as she could. "I handled it my way. You pay me to handle things my way."

Caught off guard, she stepped back. She paid him. How could she have forgotten he was only doing a job? An arrow of pain passed through her. Even that, somehow, was better than the numbness. "I expect to be kept informed of your progress, Doran."

"Fine." He picked up a piece of toast and began to heap on jelly.

"I'll just leave you to enjoy your break-fast."

"Chantel." His voice was soft, but it had enough punch to stop her before she crossed the room. "You might as well sit down. You're not going anywhere by your-self."

"I'm going down to Maddy's room."

"You can try to leave." He set his knife very deliberately on the side of his plate. "You won't make it. I'll take you down myself as soon as I'm dressed." He sent her a cool, challenging look. "And you'll stay there, inside the room, until I come back for you."

"I don't —"

"I've got a man stationed in the room across the hall, and another in the room across from your sister's. You're perfectly safe inside, but I want to take you down myself."

She was almost angry enough to take her chances. Chantel measured the distance to the door, and the look in Quinn's eyes. Without a word, she dropped down onto a chair and ignored him while he finished his breakfast.

Quinn found the cramped little flower shop in the West Sixties. In spite of the air-conditioning, the air was sultry inside and heavy with a barrage of floral scents. Three customers were crowded in, two of them in front of a long, chipped counter covered with scraps of papers and a shrilling phone the harried little man behind the counter ignored. Another customer stood in front of a display window and studied arrangements.

"Can't have them there before four. Can't." The owner scrawled on a form and kept shaking his head. He took a credit card and ran it through a machine for authorization. "Yes, it'll be pretty," he answered to the customer's murmured question. "Big pink carnations, some sprays of baby's breath. Tasteful, very tasteful. Sign here."

Quinn wandered to a grouping of lilies while the man dealt with the other customers.

"Okay, okay, you want to buy flowers or just look at them?"

Quinn glanced over to see the man piling the papers on the counter. "Pretty busy today."

"You're telling me nothing." The little man pulled out a handkerchief to wipe the back of his neck. "Got problems with the air conditioner, my clerk gets appendicitis, and too many people are dying." When Quinn lifted a brow, the man settled down a bit. "Funerals. Got a run on gladiolas this week."

"Tough." Quinn skirted a spray of daisies in a watering can. "This one of yours?"

He glanced at the card in Quinn's hand. "Says so right there." The man's squat finger punched at the name. "Flowers by Bernstein. I'm Bernstein. You have a problem with a delivery?"

"A question. Red roses, a dozen, delivered to the Plaza this morning. Who bought them?"

"You ask me who bought them?" Bernstein gave a long, nasal laugh. "Young man, I sell twenty dozen roses this week if I sell one. How am I supposed to know who buys?"

"You keep records?" Quinn gestured toward the register. "Receipts. You should have a receipt for a dozen red roses delivered to the Plaza at, let's say, ten-thirty, eleven this morning."

"You want me to go through my receipts?"

Quinn reached in his pocket and drew out a twenty. "That's right."

The little man stood straight. His drooping jowls quivered with indignation. "I don't take bribes. You got twenty dollars, you buy twenty dollars' worth of flowers."

"Fine. How about the receipts?"

"You a cop?"

"Private."

Bernstein hesitated. Then, grumbling, he went into the drawer that held the day's receipts. He mumbled to himself as he flipped through them. "Nobody bought red roses today."

"Yesterday."

That earned Quinn a disgusted look, but

Bernstein went into another drawer. "Red roses to Maine, two dozen to Pennsylvania, a dozen to Twenty-seventh Street . . ." He mumbled out a few more addresses. "A dozen to the Plaza Hotel, suite 1203, for delivery this morning."

"Can I take a look at that?" Without waiting for an answer, Quinn plucked it out of his hand. "Paid cash."

"I got no problem taking cash."

But cash meant no signature. Quinn passed the receipt back. "What did he look like?"

"What did he look like?" The man let out another snort of laughter. "How am I going to remember what you look like tomorrow? People come in here and buy their flowers. I don't care if they got an eye in the middle of their forehead so long as their credit's good or their cash is green."

"Just think about it a minute." Quinn pulled out another twenty. "You got some great flowers here."

The florist gave him a shrewd look. "The carnations on display here are getting wilted."

"I happen to be very fond of carnations."

With a nod, the man pocketed the two twenties, then took the slightly drooping carnations from behind the glass. "I remember he said to send the roses to Chantel O'Hurley. Things were pretty busy here yesterday. They hauled my clerk out in an ambulance. My other clerk's on vacation, and we've got two weddings." Because the florist had a genuine love for flowers, he took out a plastic bottle and spritzed the carnations. "Anyhow, he says to send them to her, so I say, hey, is that the actress? You know, the wife and I go to the movies a lot. Oh, yeah, I ask him if he's from California. He was wearing a hat, one of those panama types, and dark glasses."

"What did he say?"

"I don't think he did. And don't ask me what he looked like again, 'cause I don't know. I had Mrs. Donahue in here fussing about her daughter's wedding. Rose petals — bags of 'em. Pink." He shook his head. "He was a guy, and I never saw much of his face."

"How old?"

"Could've been younger than you, could've been older. But he wasn't built so big. Nervous hands," he remembered suddenly, and in a moment of conscience added some fresh greenery to the carnations.

"Why do you say that?"

"Came in here smoking some foreign cigarette. I don't allow smoking, no matter how classy the tobacco. Not good for the flowers."

"How do you know it was foreign?"

"How do I know? How do I know? I know an American cigarette when I see one," the florist said testily. "And this wasn't one of them. Made him put it out too. Don't care how much money you spend in here, you ain't gonna pollute my flowers."

"Okay, so he had nervous hands."

"Couldn't keep them still once he put the thing out. Look, I had enough trouble in here yesterday without this character. Mrs. Donahue was driving me to grief and my clerk was getting her appendix out. Next thing you know, she'll want to claim it on workman's compensation."

"Anything else?" Quinn steered him patiently away from his clerk's appendectomy. "Anything he did or said that sticks in your mind?"

"Money clip," he said abruptly. "Yeah, he took the cash out of a clip instead of a wallet. A nice one, nothing you'd pick up on the street. Silver. Monogrammed."

"What initials?"

"Initials?" The florist began to file away his stack of receipts. "What do I know from initials? It had squiggly lines on it."

"Any rings? A watch?"

"I don't know. I notice the clip because the guy's got a nice fat wad tucked into it. Maybe he's got jewelry, maybe he doesn't. I'm taking his cash, not giving him an appraisal."

"Thanks." Quinn took out a card and wrote his number at the hotel on the back. "I'd appreciate it if you'd call if you remember anything else. Or if he comes back."

"He in trouble?"

"Let's just say I'd like the chance to talk to him."

"Don't forget your carnations."

Quinn tucked the arrangement under his arm and headed for the door.

"Guess you get some weirdos out in California," Bernstein commented.

"Our share."

"Movie stars." He gave another quick snort. "Guy said he worked close with Miss O'Hurley. Real close."

Quinn's fingers tightened around the knob. "Thanks." As he stepped onto the sidewalk, he thrust the flowers into the arms of a woman dragging a shopping cart. He didn't look back to see her staring at him. There was a sick feeling starting in his stomach. He knew someone who occasionally carried a silver money clip. A clip that had been a present from Chantel. Matt Burns.

He didn't want to believe it. Matt was a friend, and no one knew better than Quinn how hard it was to make and keep friends in his business. Yet how well did he really know Matt Burns?

He hadn't known about the gambling until he'd dug it up. Matt had betrayed a client then because of a weakness. Didn't that make him first in line to betray Chantel because of another kind of weakness?

A lot of men carried money clips, Quinn reminded himself as he headed away from the hotel rather than toward it. He needed to think things through before going back to Chantel. A lot of men carried silver money clips, Quinn continued, just the way a lot of men smoked foreign cigarettes. But he wondered how many men who knew Chantel, who worked closely with Chantel, did both.

He was being stupid, Quinn decided as he stopped at a phone booth. The word was soft, he corrected. That's what the woman had done to him. It wasn't his job to find reasons why it couldn't be Matt, but find reasons why it could.

Flipping open his notepad, he scanned for Matt's number and dialed.

"Answering for Matt Burns."

"I need to speak with him."

"I'm sorry, Mr. Burns is unavailable until Monday."

"Make him available, sweetheart. It's important."

The voice became very prim. "I'm sorry, Mr. Burns is out of town."

Nerves skimmed down Quinn's spine. "Where?"

"I'm not permitted to give out that information."

"This is Quinn Doran. I'm calling for Chantel O'Hurley."

"Oh, I'm sorry, Mr. Doran. You should have told me who you were. Mr. Burns is out of town, I'm afraid. Should I have him get in touch with you if he checks in?"

"I'll get in touch with him on Monday. Where is he?"

"He flew to New York, Mr. Doran. On some personal business."

"Yeah." He bit off an oath as he hung up the phone. It was very personal. This was going to hurt her, Quinn thought. And it was going to hurt deep.

"Three more hours." Maddy O'Hurley jumped up from her chair, paced across the room and plopped onto the sofa. "We should have gotten married in the morning."

"It'll be afternoon soon enough." Chantel sipped at her third cup of coffee and wondered when she would hear from Quinn again. "Shouldn't you be enjoying your last hours as a single woman?"

"I'm too wired to enjoy anything." Maddy was up again, her mop of red hair bouncing with the movement. "I'm so glad you're here." She stopped long enough to give Chantel a quick squeeze. "I'd be going crazy now if you weren't. I wish Abby would come down."

"She will, as soon as she dumps Dylan and the boys on Pop. Think about something else."

"Something else." Maddy's slim dancer's body spun in a circle. "How can I think of something else? Walking down that aisle is the biggest entrance I'll ever make."

"Speaking of entrances, tell me about the play."

"It's terrific." Her amber eyes lighted with love of the theater. "Maybe I'm prejudiced because it was the play that brought Reed and me together, but it's the best thing I've done. I was hoping you'd be able to see it."

"I'll be back in New York shooting on location soon. You'll be back from your honeymoon and onstage." Chantel reached restlessly for a cigarette. "And if the reviews are any indication, the thing's going to be running for years."

Maddy watched her sister toy with, then light, the cigarette. It was something she did rarely, and only when she was tense. "How's the filming going?"

"No complaints."

"And this Quinn? Is it serious?"

Chantel moved her shoulders. "He's just a man."

"Come on, Chantel, this is Maddy. I've seen you with just a man before. Did you have an argument?" She managed to keep herself still long enough to sit on the arm of Chantel's chair. "Last night you seemed so happy. You practically glowed every time you looked at him."

"Of course I'm happy." She gave Maddy's arm a quick pat. "My baby sister's getting married to a man I've decided is nearly worthy of her."

"Don't hedge, Chantel." Abruptly serious, Maddy took Chantel's restless hands in hers. Nerves seemed to leap from one sister to the other. "Hey, something's really wrong, isn't it?"

"Don't be silly, I —" She broke off at the

knock on the door. Maddy felt her sister's fingers tense.

"Chantel, what is it?"

"Nothing." Disgusted with herself, Chantel made her muscles relax. "Just make sure who it is, darling. We don't want an overexuberant bridegroom walking in."

Far from satisfied, Maddy rose and walked to the door. "It's Abby," she said as she looked through the peephole. And with Abby's help, she thought, she'd get to the bottom of what was worrying their sister. "How come you're not fat yet?" she accused as she opened the door.

With a laugh, Abby put one hand on her stomach and the other on Maddy's cheek. "Because I have over five months to go. How come you're not getting ready yet?"

"Because the wedding's not for three hours."

"Just enough time." Abby draped a garment bag over the back of a chair and went to Chantel. "Think we can whip her into shape?"

"Maybe. At least if we start on her she can't pace around the suite. Thank God Reed talked you into giving up that apartment. We'd have been sitting on top of each other."

"I still miss it." With a grin, Maddy

moved over to wrap an arm around each of her sisters. "I have such a hard time picturing me in a penthouse uptown. Are Dylan and the boys with Pop?"

"I left them at his door. Mom's getting her hair done, and Pop was about to talk Dylan into a prewedding toast. I can't wait to see Ben in his tux again. He looks like such a little man. And Chris is annoyed that we're renting them instead of buying them. He thinks it's just the thing to show off to his friends at home. And by the way —" she gave Chantel a squeeze before she released her "— I liked your Quinn."

"The possessive pronoun's a bit premature." Chantel managed a smile. Then, on impulse, she went to the phone. "I know what's missing here," she told them, punching up Room-Service. "I'd like a bottle of champagne, three glasses. Dom Pérignon '71. Yes, Madeline O'Hurley's suite. Thank you."

Abby arched a brow and leaned her arm on Maddy's shoulder. "It's barely eleven."

"Who's counting?" Chantel wanted to know. "The O'Hurley Triplets are going to celebrate." Without warning, her eyes filled. "Oh, God, sometimes I miss the two of you so much I can hardly stand it."

In an instant they were together, holding

269

close in the bond that had cemented them even before birth. Maddy sniffled, Abby soothed, and then, to her sisters' amazement, Chantel broke down completely.

"Oh, baby." Abby lowered her to the sofa, casting a quick, concerned look at Maddy. "What's wrong, Chantel?"

"It's nothing, nothing." She brushed her tears aside. "Just being sentimental. I guess I'm a little edgy, working too hard. Just seeing the two of you, you with your beautiful family, Abby, and Maddy about to start one of her own. I wonder if things had been different . . ." She let her words trail off with a shake of her head. "No, I made my choices, now I have to deal with them."

Abby brushed the hair from Chantel's face. Her voice was always calm, her hands always gentle. "Chantel, is this about Quinn?"

"Yes — No." She lifted both hands, then dropped them. "I don't know. I'm having a little trouble with an overenthusiastic fan," she said, downplaying her problem. "I hired Quinn to more or less keep him at a distance, and then I fell in love with him and . . ." She trailed off again, letting out a deep breath. "I just said it out loud."

Maddy bent down to kiss the top of her head. "Did it help?"

Some of the tension uncurled. "Maybe. I'm being an idiot." She fumbled for a tissue. "And I'll be damned if I'm going to walk down the aisle as maid of honor with puffy eyes."

"That sounds more like Chantel," Maddy murmured. "And besides, if you're in love with Quinn, everything's going to work out."

"Always the optimist."

"Absolutely. Abby found Dylan, I found Reed, so it's your turn. Now if we could just pin down Trace . . ."

"You're really reaching," Chantel said with a laugh. "If there's a woman out there who can put a hobble on big brother, I'd love to meet her." She started at the knock on the door, but brought herself back quickly. "Must be the champagne." Stuffing the tissue in her pocket, Chantel went to the door but checked the peephole first. "Uh-oh." A smile hovered on her lips as she glanced over her shoulder. "We've got the champagne, all right, but there's more. Abby, drag Maddy into the bedroom. There's a lovesick maniac at the door."

"Reed? Is it Reed?" Maddy was halfway to the door before her sisters headed her off.

"No way." She might be nearly four months pregnant, but Abby was still agile.

She had an arm hooked around Maddy's waist. "Bad luck, honey. You get into the bedroom. Chantel and I can transmit any messages."

"This is silly."

"I'm not opening the door until you're out of the room," Chantel said simply, and leaned back on it. "All the way out."

After wrinkling her nose, Maddy slammed the door behind her. As a precaution, Abby posted herself in front of it. With a nod of satisfaction, Chantel pulled open the door to the hall. "Just over there," she told the waiter. "And you —" she put a slender, manicured finger to Reed's chest "— not a step farther."

"I just want to see her for a minute."

Chantel managed to force back a smile and shook her head. She could almost feel the love coming from him, the nerves, the longing. He hadn't changed into his tux yet, and he was wearing a pair of casual slacks and a shirt that reflected his conservative style. He looked like an executive. He *was* an executive, she thought with another shake of her head. And the farthest thing from the type one would have imagined with her free-spirited, bohemian sister. Yet they fit. Chantel imagined Maddy had fallen for those calm gray eyes first. The rest would have been a smooth drop.

"Look, I have something for her." Used to getting his own way, Reed took a step forward, only to be blocked easily by Chantel. "I'll be in and out before you know it."

"You won't be in at all," Chantel corrected. "We're Irish, Reed, and we're theater people. You're not going to find a group more superstitious. You'll see Maddy at the church."

"That's right." Hearing a stirring behind her, Abby hooked her hand firmly around the knob of the bedroom door. "I'm sure you're too much of a gentleman to try to get through both of us." Using the ultimate weapon, she smiled and put a hand to her stomach. "Or should I say all three of us?"

Reed wasn't so sure. He wanted to see Maddy, touch her, if only for a minute, to assure himself it was all real. Abby smiled at him with warm, sympathetic eyes, but she didn't budge. Chantel signed the receipt for the wine without moving from the doorway.

"Go down to the eighth floor and have a drink with Pop," she advised.

"I just want to —"

"Forget it." Then she softened and kissed his cheek. "Just a couple of hours, Reed. Believe me, it'll be worth the wait."

Only minutes before, Reed had managed

to talk his way around Dylan and override Frank's objections. But he knew when he was out of his depth. "Would you give her this?" He took a small box from his pocket. "It was my grandmother's. I was going to give it to her later, but, well, I'd like her to wear it today."

"She'll wear it." She started to hustle him out again, then stopped. "Reed."

"Yeah?"

"Welcome to the family." Then she shut the door in his face. "Lord, another minute of that and I'd have been in tears again. Let her out."

"What did he give you?" Maddy was already nudging past her sister. She took the box from Chantel and opened it. Inside was a tiny heart of diamonds on a thin silver chain. "Oh, isn't it lovely?"

"It's going to look even lovelier against your dress." Abby ran a fingertip over the stones. "Here, I'll clasp it for you."

"Now *I'm* going to cry." Maddy closed her hand over the heart. He was going to be hers, truly hers, in a matter of hours. And her new life would begin.

"No more tears." Chantel released the cork from the wine with a swoosh. It landed on the carpet, to be ignored as she poured wine to overflowing into three glasses.

"We're going to get just a little drunk — Well, two of us are going to get a little drunk, and Abby's going to have half a glass. Then, between the three of us, we're going to create the most beautiful bride to ever walk down the aisle at St. Pat's. Here's to you, little sister."

"No." Maddy touched her glass to Chantel's, then to Abby's. "Here's to us. As long as we have each other, we're never alone."

Chapter Eleven

At Chantel's insistence, she and Quinn caught the red-eye to L.A. Saturday night. New York hadn't been the haven she'd hoped for. With the wedding over and her sister off on a Caribbean honeymoon, Chantel could only think of getting home.

The reception had been a strain. She'd caught herself watching strangers, studying familiar faces and wondering. Even when she willed herself to sleep on the plane, she promised herself that the next time she came back to New York, it would be without fear.

And what could she say to Quinn? She felt betrayed by his silence, yet had she, by the extent of her dependence on him, asked for it? Was she so weak, so cowardly, that he felt it necessary to shield her from everything? She wanted his protection, but she also wanted his respect. Had she forfeited that by refusing to listen to his reports, by allowing him to intercept the notes and keep the contents from her? It was time that stopped. All her life, except for one brief period, she had had her hand on the controls. Now, through fear, she'd relinquished them. Starting now, she was taking back the helm.

Quinn wondered how long it would take her to unfreeze. She'd certainly been cool enough throughout the afternoon and evening. Cool, aloof, distant. It was something he had no choice but to accept. Yet when he'd seen her walking down the aisle in front of her sister, wearing that pale blue dress, all filmy and romantic, he'd wanted to step out of his seat, scoop her up and carry her off. Somewhere. Anywhere.

He wondered what it would feel like to stand where Reed Valentine had stood, to watch Chantel, as Reed had watched Maddy, walk toward him wearing white lace. What would it be like to hear her make the promises her sister had made? He shook himself out of the mood.

They were almost ready to land, and Chantel was dozing restlessly beside him. Couldn't she understand that he'd done what he'd done for her sake, because he'd needed so badly to see her relax, even if only for a couple of days? She didn't understand, or wouldn't, and he hadn't tried to explain. He didn't know how.

He didn't have the flair of one of her leading men. He didn't have the words all neatly typed in a script he could memorize. He had only what was inside him, and there didn't seem to be a way to explain that. Words weren't feelings. Phrases weren't emotions. And emotions were all he had.

When they landed, Chantel looked fresh and rested, as though she'd spent eight hours sleeping on a soft bed rather than snatching naps on a plane. They got their luggage without incident and within twenty minutes were riding in the back of a limo toward Beverly Hills.

Chantel lighted a cigarette, then glanced casually at her watch. Right now she felt wired, restless. Jet lag would hit tomorrow, but she would function.

"I'd like to see your reports, all of your reports, by noon tomorrow."

Streetlights flashed intermittently against the windows. His face was in shadow, but Chantel doubted she would have been able to read his expression in any case. "Fine. I have the file at your place."

"I'd also like an update on anything you came up with in New York."

"You're the boss."

"I'm glad you remember that."

He could have strangled her. He thought

about ways that were quick and quiet, but instead he simply sat back and bided his time. He stepped out of the limo at the gate. Though Chantel had been gone, he'd thought it best to leave the twenty-four-hour guard in place. A few brief words and he was back in the limo, gliding through the open gates.

At the entrance, Chantel sailed past him. She had reached the head of the main staircase before he caught her.

"Something eating you, angel?"

"I don't know what you're talking about. You will excuse me now, Quinn?" Delicately she peeled his fingers from her arm. "I want to take a long, hot bath."

No one did it better. He had to give her that as he watched her walk down the hall to her room. She could, with a look, with an inflection, slice a man in half without leaving a drop of blood.

He thought he was calm. He thought he was controlled — until the moment he heard the lock click on her door. Then the rage he'd held in throughout the day clawed free. He didn't hesitate. Maybe he wasn't even thinking. Quinn walked to her bedroom door and kicked it in.

She wasn't often speechless. Chantel just stood there. The jacket of her suit had already been discarded, leaving her in a pale pink teddy and a rose-colored skirt. One hand remained frozen on top of her head where she had begun to pin up her hair.

She'd seen fury before, real and simulated, but she'd never seen anything like what was boiling in Quinn's eyes.

"Don't you ever lock a door on me." His voice was so quiet after the crash of splintering wood that she shivered. "Don't you ever walk away from me."

Slowly she lowered her hand so that her hair tumbled to her shoulders. "I want you to leave."

"Maybe it's time you learned even you can't have everything you want. I'm here to stay. You're going to have to do a hell of a lot more than turn a key to keep me out."

When he came toward her, she stiffened but refused to retreat. She was through backing away from anything, even him. He took her hair and wrapped it around his hand.

"You wanted to slap me down, and that's fine. But I'll be damned if I'll take it from you for doing my job."

"I won't be treated like a fool, or a weakling." The lace of the teddy trembled over her breasts as she took an unsteady breath. "You knew he was going to follow me to

New York. You knew I'd be no safer there than I was here."

"That's right. I knew, you didn't. And you had one night when you didn't toss in your sleep."

"You had no right —"

"I had every right." The hand in her hair tightened. She wanted to wince, but she didn't seem to be able to move at all. "I have the right to do anything, everything, to keep you safe, to give you some peace of mind. And I'm going to keep on doing it, because there's nothing that matters to me more than you."

Chantel let out a breath she hadn't been aware of holding. She'd seen it in his eyes, beneath the anger, beneath the frustration, but she hadn't been certain she could believe it. "Is that your —" She stopped, pressing her lips together. It wouldn't do for her voice to tremble now. She wanted to be strong, for him, as well as herself. "Is that your way of telling me you love me?"

He stared down at her, a good deal more stunned by his announcement than she. He hadn't meant to throw it at her like a threat. He'd wanted to give them both time, to give them both room, so that he could coax her along until she realized she needed him. But he'd never been good at coaxing.

"Take it or leave it."

"Take it or leave it," she repeated in a murmur. How like him. "Would you mind letting go of my hair? I need it for a couple of scenes on Monday. Besides, that way you'd have both arms to put around me."

Before he could, she was pressed against him, holding tight and hard and praying it wasn't a dream.

"I guess this means you're taking it." He buried his face in her hair and wondered how he'd ever survived without her scent, without her touch.

"Yeah. I've been trying to figure out a way to make you fall in love with me so you wouldn't be able to walk away." She tossed her head back to look at him. "Tell me you're not going to walk away."

"I'm not going anywhere." Then he found her mouth and made it a promise. "Let me hear you say it." He took her hair again but drew it back gently until their eyes met. "Look at me and say it. No lights, no camera, no script."

"I love you, Quinn, more than I thought it was possible to love. It scares the hell out of me."

"Good." He kissed her again, harder. "It scares the hell out of me, too."

"We've got so many things to talk about."

"Later." He was already drawing down the zipper of her skirt.

"Later," she agreed, tugging his shirt out of the waistband of his slacks. "Want to take a bath?" As she asked, she yanked his shirt over his shoulders.

"Yeah."

"Before?" With a laugh, she nipped at his chin. "Or after?"

"After." And he pulled her with him onto the bed.

It had been wild before, fierce, violent, passionate, and it had also shimmered with gentleness. But now there was love, felt, spoken, answered. She'd stopped believing that her life would lead her to this — love, acceptance, understanding. In the end she'd only had to open her hand and take it. In a burst of emotion they were caught close, mouths open and hungry, bodies heated and aware. She heard his long indrawn breath as he buried his face in her hair, as if he, too, had just realized what a gift they'd been given.

She thought he trembled. Her hands, pressed against his back, felt the quick tensing of muscle. She didn't want to soothe it. She wanted him to be as she was, stunned, a little afraid, and deliriously happy. When she pressed her lips to his throat she felt the throb of excitement, tasted the heat. In one long, possessive stroke she ran her hands down his back, then up again. He was hers. From this moment, he was hers.

She was there for him, soft, yielding, yet strong enough to hold him. He'd never looked for her. Quinn understood himself well enough to know he'd never looked for anyone to share his life. Still, he'd found her, and in her he'd found everything. A mate. There was something primitive yet soothing in the word. It meant someone to tumble between the sheets with on hot, sultry nights. It meant someone to wake with in the cool, lazy mornings. It was someone to confide in, someone to protect, someone to reach out to.

Just the thought of it made him close his eyes, as if to keep the fantasy trapped forever. With his fingertips he traced her face so that her image hovered there, in his mind.

"So beautiful," he murmured. "Here . . ." His finger lingered on her cheek. "And here." Slowly he slid his hand down her body. Then he opened his eyes to look into hers. "And inside."

"No, I —"

"Don't contradict the man who loves

you." He brought her palm to his lips, watching her. He turned her hand over, kissing each finger. The diamond glittered on one, a symbol of what she was to the world. Cool sex, glamour with a hard polish. Her hand trembled like a young girl's.

He brushed kisses along her jawline, and her breath came in slow, quiet gasps. She could almost hear her skin hum as his fingers whispered over it. With each touch she drifted deeper into a dark, liquid world where sensations were her only guide.

Only he could make her forget the boundaries she'd once set for herself. Only he could make her forget that when you loved, you risked. With him she could be without fear, without reservations or restrictions. There would be a tomorrow with Quinn. There would be a lifetime of tomorrows.

He wasn't sure he knew how to show her how he felt. He wasn't used to pampering. Romance was for books, for movies, for the young and foolish. Yet he had a need, a growing one, to show her that his feelings went so far beyond desire that he couldn't measure them.

Rising to his elbow, he brushed the hair carefully away from her face, combing his fingers through it as it fell, silvery-blond, over the spread. Gently, as though she might crumble at the slightest touch, he cupped her face in his hand. Could she be more beautiful now? Somehow it seemed so to him as he watched the first beams of daylight steal through the windows and over her skin.

He ran his thumb over her lips, fascinated by the shape, by the softness, by the flavor he imagined would linger on his own flesh. As if it were the first time — and perhaps it was — he touched his lips to hers.

Her body went weak. As his lips lingered, the hand she had pressed to his back slipped down, limp. She'd thought she understood possession, but she'd been wrong. She'd thought she could imagine what it was like to be loved, loved fully. But she'd had no idea. Something fluttered through her, so softly that it might have been a dream. But it expanded within her, and a promise was made.

The heat centered, focused and grew. Strength flooded back into her, and with it a passion so rich that she moaned from the pleasure. Together they rolled until she lay over him. Together they let themselves go.

His hands were quick, but no more urgent than hers. His lips were hungry, but his desperation had met its match. Sanity was discarded as easily as silk and lace. They came together like thunder, in a storm that lingered into the morning. As dawn rose, they took each other into the dark.

"I'm so glad it's Sunday." Chantel eased her shoulders down into the hot, frothy water. She picked up a wineglass from the side of the tub and laughed at Quinn over the rim. "You're not supposed to scowl at the bubbles. You're supposed to enjoy them."

Quinn shifted to reach for his own glass. Chantel's tub was easily big enough for two, and the skylight overhead showed a perfect blue sky. The water that lapped nearly to the edge was layered with white, fragrant bubbles.

"I'm going to smell like a woman."

"Darling." She touched her tongue to the rim of her glass. "No one's going to smell you but me."

"With all the stuff you dumped in here, I'll be lucky if it wears off in a week." He shifted again, and his leg slid over hers. "But it has its compensations."

"Mmmm." With her eyes half closed, she leaned back. "For both of us. I need this. The shooting schedule next week is murder. There are three scenes in particular that I know will leave me limp. The one where Brad and Bailey nearly die in the fire is the worst."

"What fire?"

"Read the script," she said lazily, smiling when he tossed bubbles at her. "I trust Special Effects, but it doesn't make it any easier to crawl around in a shack on the back lot or on the set on the soundstage while they're shooting flames and pumping smoke in. That's why it's especially nice that it's Sunday and I can lie in the tub and think about making love with you." She looked at him through eyes that were hardly more than slits. "Again."

"You can lie in the tub *and* make love with me." He twisted his body, bringing it forward until his face was close to hers. "At the same time."

Chantel laughed and linked her hands behind his head as water lapped over the tub and onto the floor. "Too much water."

"You filled it up."

"My mistake. I usually bathe alone."

"Not anymore." Bubbles burst between them as he kissed her. "Why don't you pull the plug?"

"Can't get to it." She tilted her head to change the angle of the next kiss. "It's, ah, behind me. Now I bet a big strong man like you could manage it all by himself."

"Back here?" His hand trailed over her breast, then slipped to her rib cage.

"Close. Very close." She felt his fingers slide over her hip. "Getting closer. Why don't we —" The words were cut off as she found herself submerged, his mouth hard on hers. Up again, she drew in air, swiped at her face and squinted at him. "Quinn!"

"Slipped." He found the lever easily and flipped it down.

"I bet. Now I've got soap in my eyes." He started to grin, but his mouth went dry when she rose up, magnificent, and let water drain from her skin as she reached for a towel. "Remind me to bring a snorkel next time we take a bath."

"Chantel."

She was holding the towel to her face, but she lowered it with a half smile that faded when he stood beside her. Without a word, he gathered her to him. They stood where they were while the bubbles drained beneath them and dried on their skin.

"I never knew it could be like this," she murmured. "Not like this."

"That makes two of us." He'd found her. It seemed so incredible that he'd found her, found everything, without looking. "You're getting cold." Feeling the chill on her skin, he took a towel and wrapped it around her. "I guess I'd have a lot to answer to if you went to work tomorrow with a red nose."

"I never get a red nose." She took a towel in turn and wrapped it around him. "It's in my contract."

"Think you could take a break when you finish filming?"

"That depends." She smiled again. "On where and with whom."

"With me. We can talk about the where."

"I should be wrapped in three weeks. You pick the where." She started to step from the tub, then braced herself against the wall. "Careful. We've flooded the place."

"Just toss down a couple towels." Quinn plucked another from the shelf and let it fall to the floor to soak up the water.

"My housekeeper's going to love you." Out of habit, Chantel picked up a jar of moisturizer and began to rub a light cover over her skin.

"After we're married, there's going to have to be a change in the rules of the tub." He was hooking the towel at his waist and didn't notice the way her fingers froze in place on her cheek. "Bubbles are okay, but they've got to be unscented. It's one thing for the staff to sniff, but we can't have the kids wondering if their father wears perfume."

Somehow she managed to get the lid back on the jar and set it down without dropping it. "We're getting married?"

He didn't have to look at her to know she'd taken three paces back. He heard it in her voice. "Absolutely."

Her heart was hammering in her throat, but she'd trained herself to speak clearly over nerves. "You want children?"

"Yeah." One by one, the muscles of his stomach knotted. "Is that a problem?"

"I . . . Things are moving pretty fast," she managed.

"We're not teenagers, Chantel. I think we both know what we want."

"I have to sit down." She didn't trust her legs, so she moved quickly back to the bedroom and took a chair. She held the towel together in front of her with hands that had gone white at the knuckles.

Quinn waited a moment. The steam had fogged the wall-length mirror opposite the tub, but he could imagine her sitting there, her beauty reflected, slim, young, perfect. She was a dream and, more, she was a star, someone who lighted up the screen and created fantasies. His jaw was tight when he walked into the bedroom.

"Looks like I pushed the wrong buttons." Digging up his shirt, he found his cigarettes.

"I thought that's what you wanted, too." Lighting one, he drew smoke in deeply. "I guess a husband and kids don't go with the image."

She looked up slowly. Her eyes were dry, but he recognized pain, something deep and dull and lasting.

"Chantel —"

"No." She stopped him with a gesture of her hand. "Maybe I deserved that." Rising, she went to the closet and chose a robe. With deliberate motions she dropped the towel, then slipped the robe on and belted it. She linked her fingers a moment, then let them fall to her sides. "My career is important to me, but I've never let it interfere with my personal life — or vice versa. My work is demanding. You've seen for yourself that the hours can be brutal."

"So there's no room for me and a family?"

Something came into her face again. Pain again, but with a touch of anger this time. "My parents raised four children on the road. There was always room, always time for family."

"Then what is it?"

She dipped her hands into her pockets, then took them out again, unable to keep them still. "First, I want to tell you that there's nothing I want more than to marry you and start a family. Please, don't," she said quickly when he started to come to her. "Sit down, Quinn. It would be easier for me if you would sit."

"All right."

When he had, she drew a deep breath. "There are things you have to know before we go any farther. It's difficult, at least for me, to admit past mistakes, but you have a right to know. If I'd listened to my mother, I would have told you before. It might have been easier then."

"Look, if you want to tell me you've been with other men —"

Her low laugh cut him off. It was strained. "Not exactly. This doesn't fit the image, either, but I only slept with one other man before you. Surprise," she said quietly when he simply stared. She went to stand at the window. "I was barely twenty when I met him. I was doing commercials, going to acting classes. I even had a part-time job selling magazines on the phone. I kept telling myself it was just a matter of time, and I believed it, but it was tough. Oh, God, it was so tough to be alone. Then Matt called and said he'd gotten me a test for a small part on a feature. *Lawless*, my first real break. The producer was —"

"Dustin Price."

Chantel turned back from the window. Her hand was curled in a fist. "Yes. How do you know that?"

"A lot of movie buffs might, but the fact is, I already know about Price. He turned up when I did a background check on you."

"You did a check on me?" She found herself braced against the windowsill. "On me?"

"It's standard, Chantel. I do a run on you, maybe somebody turns up you've forgotten, or forgotten to mention. Like Dustin Price. He's clean, by the way. Been in England eighteen months."

"Standard," she repeated, letting the rest sift away like sand. "I guess I should have expected it."

"What difference does it make now? So you slept with him. You needed a break, he could give you a break. It was years ago, and I don't give a damn."

Every muscle in her body went rigid. "Is that what you think? You think I slept with him to get a part?"

"I'm telling you I don't care."

"Don't touch me." She whipped away from him as he reached for her. "I don't have to sleep with anyone to get a part, and I never have. I may have made compromises. I may have given up more than I should, but

I never prostituted myself."

"I'm sorry." This time he took her arms, ignoring her resistance. "I'm trying to tell you that whatever happened between you and Price doesn't matter."

"Oh, it matters." She pulled away and poured wine into a fresh glass. "It matters. When Matt called me to tell me I had the part, I was so happy. I knew it was the beginning. I was going places. I was going to be somebody." She pressed her fingers to her lips until she was sure she could speak calmly. "Dustin sent me a dozen roses, a bottle of champagne and a lovely letter of congratulations. He said he knew I was going to be a star and suggested we have dinner to discuss the film and my career."

She drank because her throat was dry, then set down the glass, refusing to rely on wine to get her through the story. "Of course, I agreed. He was one of the top producers, riding on a wave of three box-office smashes. Of course, he was married, but I didn't think of that." The derision was in her voice again, self-derision, self-disgust.

"Chantel. It was years ago."

"There are some things you never stop paying for. I was going to be sophisticated. We were just having dinner, colleagues. God, he was charming." The memory still hurt, but the pain was dull now, covered with scar tissue. "The flowers kept coming, the dinners. He knew so much about the business, the people. Who to talk to, who to be seen with. All of that was so important to me then. I thought I could handle it. The truth was I was just a naive young girl on her own for the first time.

"I fell in love with him. I believed everything he said about him and his wife living together for appearances only, about the quiet divorce that was already in the works. About the two of us making the best and brightest team Hollywood had seen since the golden age. The whole thing might have run its natural course as I got a little smarter, and he a bit bored, but before all that happened, I made a mistake." She ran her damp palms down her robe, then linked them. "I got pregnant." She managed to swallow. "You didn't find that in your background check, did you?"

Rage hit, and he smothered it. "No."

"He had enough money, enough influence, to keep it quiet. And it wasn't an issue for very long."

He was struggling, fighting desperately to understand. "You had an abortion?"

"That's what he wanted. He was furious. I suppose a lot of men would be when their mistress — and that's what I was, really — turns up pregnant and threatens his very comfortable marriage. Of course, he'd never planned on getting a divorce or marrying me. All of that came out when I told him I was going to have his baby."

"He used you," Quinn spit out. "You were twenty years old and he used you."

"No." Strange that she could say it so calmly now. "I was twenty years old and I pretended I knew all the rules. I pretended very well. I made one mistake, then I made another mistake. I told him he could go to hell, but I was keeping the baby. Things got ugly then. He threatened to destroy my career if I didn't play his way. Well, there's no use going into what was said, except that the affair was over and my eyes were wide open."

"You're still hurting," Quinn said quietly.

"Yes, but not for the reasons you might think. I thought I loved him, but as soon as the glitter washed off I knew I never had. I called my parents. I was ready to run home and leave everything behind. I bought plane tickets. Quinn, I don't know what I would have ultimately done once I was thinking clearly. That's the worst of it, not knowing. There was an accident on the way to the airport." She took a deep breath, struggling to finish. "Nothing major, the taxi driver had a couple of broken bones, and I — I lost the baby."

With a broken sob, she pressed her fingers to her eyes. "I lost the baby, and I tried to tell myself it was for the best. But all I ever could think was that it had never had a chance. I was only six weeks pregnant. Six weeks. Here, then gone. Matt pulled me out of it, got me back to work almost as soon as I was out of the hospital. Everything clicked for me then, the parts, the people, the fame I'd always wanted. All I had to do was lose a baby."

"Chantel." He came to her, running his hands over her face, her hair, her shoulders. "There's nothing I can say. Nothing I know how to do."

"There's more."

"No more." He started to gather her close, but she backed away.

"When I lost the baby, there were complications. The doctors told me, well, they said it was possible I could have other children, but it wasn't something they could guarantee. Possible, just possible, not even probable. There might never be another baby, another chance. Do you understand?"

He took her hands. "Are you going to marry me?"

"Quinn, aren't you listening? I just told you —"

"I heard you." His fingers linked with hers and held firm. "You might not be able to have children. I want them, Chantel — yours, mine. If we can have them, that's great. But first, always . . ." He bent to touch his lips to hers. "I want you. I need you, angel. The rest is up to chance."

"Quinn, I love you."

"Then let's get married tomorrow."

"No." She put her hands to his chest to hold him off. "I want you to think about this, really think about it. You need some time."

"I need you," he corrected. "I don't need time."

"I feel I owe it to you. Let's leave things as they are. A few days."

He could have pushed. He could have won. But the hurt seemed too close to the surface just then. "A very few days. Come here." This time she went willingly into his arms. "I'm not going to let anyone hurt you again," he murmured.

She closed her eyes, hoping she could promise him the same thing, even if she were speaking of herself.

Chapter Twelve

The day started at six and never let up. Filming began at a shack on the back lot. The interior was no more than that, a small frame building that had been used in a handful of films. For *Strangers* it had been given a face-lift, a false front that had turned it into a rustic cabin in the woods of New England. In a climactic scene, Special Effects would burn it down, the fire starting under mysterious circumstances with Hailey and Brad inside.

The interior scenes would be shot later, on a two-story set on the soundstage, but the morning was spent on exteriors. Chantel drove Hailey's Ferrari to the deserted cabin. She was older now, but still caught between the man she had married and the man who had betrayed her. The scene called for her, on the verge of a breakdown, to seek solace in the remote cabin, searching for the roots of her art, which she'd lost in the tangle of success.

All the scenes were shot out of sequence

and then would be edited together. For several hours of this shoot there was no dialogue. She was filmed unloading her art equipment, setting an easel on the narrow porch, walking through the door and out again with costume changes. There was a long, lingering close-up of her leaning on the porch rail with a cup of coffee in her hand. Without words, Chantel could use only her face to show the turmoil her character was feeling.

She painted on the porch, sketched on the porch steps, planted flowers. Through posture and gestures and by relaxing the set of her face, Chantel showed her character's gradual healing.

From the sidelines, Quinn watched her and felt his pride in her grow. He didn't know the story, but he understood the woman she became for the cameras. And he began to root for Hailey.

There was a poignant scene in which Hailey sat on the porch and poured out her heart to a stray dog. It was the examination of a life, with all its flaws, its wrong turns, its regrets. Even when it was reshot to change the angle, the emotion generated remained intense. Quinn saw more than one member of the crew wipe their eyes.

Before lunch they had wrapped a number

of scenes, including a short, vicious argument between Hailey and Brad on the porch. During an hour's break Chantel took a quick, necessary nap, then shored up her energy with fruit, cheese and a protein drink before going to the soundstage for the interiors.

The set was as rustic as the outside of the cabin had promised, but there were a few of Hailey's paintings on the wall. The props included a large carved music box that had been a wedding present from her husband. The earlier tension was back in her character as Chantel opened the box and let the strains of the *Moonlight-Sonata* out.

Dissatisfied with the way the scene was going, Chantel and the director went into a discussion on mood and motion.

"What do you think of our little story?" James Brewster appeared beside Quinn. The two of them watched Larry Washington bring Chantel a glass of juice.

"Hard to say when you see it chopped up this way." Quinn kept his eye on Larry as the young man hovered around Chantel, ready to jump at the tiniest gesture. "But I expect it'll sell. It has it all — sex, violence, melodrama."

"You don't write a best seller by leaving them out," Brewster said easily. "Of course,

Hailey is the key, the hinge. What she does, what she feels, affects every character. When I started the book, I thought I was telling a tale of betrayal and birth. But it became a story of how one woman — and what happens to her — determines the destiny of everyone she touches." He broke off with a laugh. "It sounds pretentious, and perhaps it would be without Chantel. She is Hailey."

"She does make you believe," Quinn murmured.

"Exactly." Pleased, Brewster gave a quick nod. "As a writer, there's no greater reward than watching one of your characters come to life, particularly one you feel strongly about. I nearly killed her in the fire, you know."

Quinn stiffened. "What do you mean?"

Brewster laughed again and drew out a cigarette. "You're a very literal man, Mr. Doran. I meant I nearly ended the book here, in this cabin, with Hailey losing everything, including her life, in a fire set by the only man who really loved her. I found it impossible. She had to go on, you see, and survive."

They both watched as the stage was set for the next take. "An extraordinary woman," Brewster murmured. "Every man here is just a little bit in love with her."

"And you?"

A wry smile in his eyes, Brewster turned. "I'm a writer, Mr. Doran. I deal in fantasies. Chantel is very much flesh and blood."

At the assistant director's signal, the set fell silent and filming began again.

Quinn watched Brewster carefully. The writer seemed less nervous than he had in the early days of shooting. Perhaps he was pleased with the progress. It was Larry Washington who seemed on edge now. Chantel's assistant was never still for long, was always moving from one spot for the next. Did the tension Quinn felt on the set come from him? It was there, Quinn sensed it sparking the air, something nervy and desperate. Yet, everywhere he looked, people were going about their jobs with the drum-tight efficiency the director insisted on.

Perhaps the tension was just within himself. There was plenty of cause. Chantel was still just out of reach, not yet ready, or not yet able, to commit herself. When a man who had lived his life avoiding commitments finally found one he wanted, he was bound to be impatient. So Quinn told himself as he watched Chantel listen to the music box with pain and indecision in her eyes.

Were her thoughts on him, he wondered, or was she in character? Her talent made it nearly impossible to separate the actress from the role.

Every eye was on her, but she was alone, in a cabin in the woods, at a turning point in her life.

"Cut. Print. Wonderful." Mary Rothschild straightened from her position behind the camera operator. "Really wonderful, Chantel."

"Thanks." She drew a deep breath and tried to shake off the emotion that had carried her through the scene. "I'm glad I don't have to do that again."

"We're going to go to the confrontation with Brad." As she spoke, Mary began to knead Chantel's shoulders. "You know what you're feeling. You still want him. After everything he's done, everything you know, you can't quite remove yourself from the young woman who fell in love with him. You want to love your husband, you've tried, but the only thing you've managed to do is hurt him. You're on the edge of your life here. You know if you go with Brad you'll never survive. Yet you're drawn."

"I'm fighting myself more than him."

"Exactly. Let's run through it."

They worked until six. Before it was over,

Special Effects had pumped smoke onto the set. Hailey, dazed by the smoke, terrified of the fire that had begun to roar through the cabin, crawled along the wooden floor in a desperate search for the door. All she carried was the music box.

"Hell of a day," Quinn commented later when they were in Chantel's trailer.

"Tell me about it." Weary, she creamed off the streaks of soot Makeup had smeared her face with. "I don't even want to eat, just sleep."

"I'll tuck you in."

She smiled and, after drying her face, swung her bag over her shoulder. "Tuck me in? I prefer having someone to snuggle against."

"You'll have that, too, in a few hours." They walked out of the trailer, past the soundstage, where the director and cinematographer were having an impromptu meeting.

"Going somewhere?"

"I've got some business." He thought of Matt, his friend, and of Chantel, the woman he loved. "I'll tell you about it when I get back."

"I'd rather you told me now." When they were outside, Chantel headed straight for the waiting limo. "Quinn, I don't want to be protected this way. Not anymore."

She was right, and he'd known that sooner or later he'd have to tell her. When she settled into the limo, he slid his arm behind, ready to comfort her.

"I didn't want to get into it in New York. You had your sister's wedding, and we had our own problems to deal with. Yesterday . . ." He hesitated, still not sure how to describe what that one twenty-four-hour-period had meant to him. "I wanted yesterday for both of us."

"I understand." She lifted a hand to his. "So, what is it, Quinn?"

"I got a lead on the man who ordered the flowers." He felt her tense, but didn't try to soothe her. She wouldn't want soothing now. "He paid cash, so there's no record. The florist couldn't give me much of a description. The guy wore dark glasses and a hat. There were a couple things the florist noticed, though." He hesitated, hating to be the one to destroy a trust and a friendship. She was more important than both. Than anything. "He smoked a foreign brand of cigarette and carried a monogrammed silver money clip."

For a moment her mind was blank. Slowly, the meaning came through. Rather than disillusionment, he saw a quick flash of determination. "A lot of men prefer foreign tobacco and clips."

"A lot of men don't work closely with you. This one said he did."

"He could have been lying."

"Could have been. We both know he wasn't. All along, the one thing we could bank on was that this man knows you, and you know him. Chantel, you gave a silver money clip to someone who works with you."

"It's not Matt."

"Angel, it's time to separate what you want from what is, or at least what might be."

"It doesn't matter what you say. I won't believe it."

"I called Matt while we were in New York." He lifted a hand to cup her face. His grip was firm. "He was out of town, Chantel."

"So he was out of town." There was a quick flutter just beneath her heart, but she ignored it. "A lot of people go out of town on weekends."

"He was in New York on personal business."

She paled, but just as quickly shook her head.

"Quinn —"

"I have to go talk to him."

"I don't want you to accuse —" A look from him cut her off. "All right," she murmured, turning her head to stare out the window. "I'm not supposed to tell you how to do your job."

"That's right, angel. Look." He took her shoulder and turned her toward him. "Look at me." When she did, he swore under his breath and brushed the hair back from her face. "I don't want this to hurt you."

"You're telling me that my closest friend is your top suspect. I can't help but be hurt."

"Go home." He leaned closer and touched his lips to hers. "Go to bed. Stop thinking about it tonight. For me," he said before she could speak. "I love you, Chantel."

"Stay home and show me."

"No." He caught her face in his hands. "I won't be long. And this is going to be over. I promise you that."

They went through the gate and up the long, quiet drive. "I trust you," she told him, and forced herself to relax. "I'm going to wait for you."

"Wait for me in bed," he murmured, hoping for her sake that she'd fall asleep quickly.

They stepped out of the limo. "You'll be careful?"

"I'm always careful."

She started up the steps, then stopped and turned back. "I hate this, but I can't regret it anymore, because it brought you. Come back soon." She walked into the house without looking back.

She wouldn't think. The day's work had drained her body, and she would concentrate on that. She'd have a late supper brought upstairs when Quinn came back. For now, she would wind down with a swim and a whirlpool.

If it was Matt, it could all be over tonight. Over. For a moment, her hope centered there. Abruptly she felt the sickness hit the pit of her stomach. No, she wouldn't wish for that. Running away from her own thoughts, she hurried upstairs to change.

"I'm glad I caught you in."

"Even superagents don't party every night." Matt was dressed in a casual sweater and slacks and comfortable boat shoes and was wound tight as a spring. "Actually, I'm having a quiet dinner at home tonight. I didn't expect to see you. Want a drink?"

"No. Thanks."

Matt set the decanter down. "How's Chantel?"

"She's fine." Rather, he was going to see that she was fine, no matter what he had to do. "Funny, I thought you'd be checking a bit more closely on that yourself."

"I figured she'd be in good hands with you." Matt rocked back and forth on his heels, not sitting, not offering Quinn a chair. "And I've been a little tied up on some personal business."

"The business take you into New York over the weekend?"

"New York?" Matt's brows drew together. "What makes you think that?"

"The florist got a pretty good look." Quinn drew out a cigarette, watching Matt as he lighted it.

"Yeah?" With a half laugh, Matt finally sat. "What the hell are you talking about, Quinn?"

"The roses you sent to Chantel. You made a mistake this time. The envelope for the card had the florist's name on it."

"Roses I sent?" Matt dragged a hand through his hair as he shook his head. "I don't know what you're getting at. I —" He stopped then, as understanding came into his eyes. "Good God, you think I've been doing this to her? You think it's me? Damn

311

it, Quinn." He sprang out of the chair. "I thought we knew each other."

"So did I. Where'd you spend the weekend, Matt?"

"None of your damn business."

Blowing out smoke, Quinn remained in his chair. "You can tell me, or I can find out. Either way, I'm going to see to it that you're out of her life."

Fury showed in clenched fists. Quinn glanced at them, almost hoping Matt would put them to use. A physical outlet would be more to his taste than this psychological sparring, hoping to wear down his opponent's resistance. "I'm her agent, I'm her friend. When she hit rock bottom, I was there for her. If I'd had those kind of feelings, I could have acted on them then."

"Where were you over the weekend?" Quinn demanded, determined to play this through to the bitter end.

"I was out of town," Matt snapped. "Personal business."

"You've had a lot of personal business going lately. You haven't shown up at all during the filming. You're such a good friend of Chantel's, but you've only seen her twice since you found out what was going on."

Guilt flashed briefly in his eyes, but then

temper obscured it. "If Chantel had wanted me, she would have called me."

"I wonder if it's you who's been calling her."

"You're crazy." But Matt's hands shook a bit as he went to pour a drink.

"You use a money clip, Matt. A silver one," Quinn continued. "One Chantel gave you. The florist picked up on a couple little details like that."

"You want to see my money clip?" Furious, Matt reached into his pocket and yanked out a wad of bills held together by a small metal clip. It hit the table with a quiet thud.

Frowning, Quinn picked it up. It was gold, not silver, with Matt's initials engraved on it.

"I've been using that for two months, since you're so interested. Ever since Marion gave it to me." He picked up his drink and tossed it back. "If it wasn't for Chantel, I'd take a shot at tossing you out."

"You're entitled to try." Quinn dropped the clip again. "Maybe you'd be smarter to level with me. Where were you over the weekend, Matt?"

"New York." Swearing, he walked to the window and back. "Brooklyn. From Friday night until Sunday afternoon — I was meeting Marion's parents. Marion Lawrence, a twenty-four-year-old schoolteacher. Twenty-four," he repeated under his breath, rubbing a hand over his face. "I met her about three months ago. She's twelve years younger than me, bright, innocent, trusting. I should have walked away. Instead, I fell in love with her." After sending Quinn a furious look, he fumbled for a cigarette of his own.

"I've spent the last three months thinking about how I relate to houses with picket fences. This young, beautiful woman is going to marry me, and I spent the weekend trying to convince her conservative and very concerned parents that I wasn't some Hollywood playboy out to take their daughter for a ride. I'd rather have faced a firing squad." He puffed on his cigarette without inhaling.

"Listen, Quinn, if I haven't been around as much as Chantel needed, it was because I've lost my head over an elementary school teacher. Look at her." Matt flipped a photograph out of his billfold. "She looks like she could still *be* in school. I've been living on nerves for weeks."

Quinn believed him. With a mixture of relief and frustration, Quinn shut the billfold. It could have been a lie, but one man in love easily recognizes another. "What the hell does she see in you?"

Matt gave a shaky laugh. "She thinks I'm terrific. She knows about the gambling, about everything, and she thinks I'm terrific. I want to marry her before she finds out any different."

"Good luck."

"Yeah." Matt put the billfold away. His temper was gone, as were his embarrassment and his nerves. But guilt remained. "If we've got that straightened out, I'd like you to fill me in about Chantel. This character sent her flowers in New York?"

"That's right."

"He looked like me?"

"I don't know what he looked like."

"But you said —"

"I lied."

"You always were a bastard," Matt said without heat. "How's she holding up?"

"She's struggling. She's going to be better knowing you're clear."

"Let me ride out with you." He rubbed the back of his neck. "I would've told her about Marion before, but I felt — I guess I felt like an idiot. Here lies Matt Burns, agent of the stars, knocked unconscious by a woman who helps kids tie their shoelaces all day."

★ ★ ★

With her hair wet and loose, Chantel came into the poolhouse after a quick swim. The water and exercise had helped clear her head. Now all she wanted was to soothe her body. Hitting the switch for the whirlpool, she sent the bubbles gushing. A sigh of gratitude purred out as she lowered her body into the hot, churning water.

Quinn would be back soon, and one way or the other they would work things out. She had to concentrate on that, and not on the circumstances that had brought them together. Not on the circumstances that had taken him away tonight.

Beams from the setting sun came through the ribbon of high windows. The skylights above were deep blue with early evening. Chantel let the jets of water beat the fatigue out of her muscles and soothe the lingering tension from her limbs.

She was on the verge of having everything she wanted. She had only to say yes to Quinn. He loved her. Chantel closed her eyes on that thought. He loved her for what she was, not what she appeared to be on the surface. No one but her family had ever accepted her totally, with her flaws, her insecurities, her mistakes. Quinn did. A woman could live a lifetime and not find a man who loved what she was on the inside.

What held her back from taking what she needed was the fear that she might not be able to give him everything — not a family of his own.

She wanted children. His children. What if she ultimately disappointed him that way? What if he, too, had to pay for her past mistakes? If she didn't love him so much, it would be so easy to say yes.

She wanted him to come back, to be with her now. If he could just hold her now, she'd know, somehow, the right answer to give him. Chantel closed her eyes and let herself sink a little deeper. When he came back to her she would know, and whatever she did would be right for both of them.

She heard a sound, a soft one, at the back of the poolhouse. Straightening, Chantel pushed the wet hair away from her face. "Quinn? Don't say anything now." She closed her eyes again. "Just come here."

Then she heard the music, and her heart shot to her throat.

It was quiet, lovely, with the bell-like quality only the best music boxes achieve. The sky was nearly dark as the strains of the *Moonlight-Sonata* flowed over the sound of churning water.

"Quinn." But she said his name knowing

he wasn't there. Her hand shook as she reached over and turned off the jets. In the silence, the music box continued to play. Putting the heels of her hands behind her, Chantel pushed herself out of the tub.

"I've waited so long for this."

At the whisper, the air clogged in her throat. She had to breathe, she told herself. If she was to get to the door she had to breathe, and the door was so far away. The lights dimmed, and the fear raced along her skin.

"You're so beautiful. So incredibly beautiful. Nothing I could imagine or create could be as perfect. Tonight, we'll finally be together."

He was in the shadows near the rear door. Chantel forced herself to look, but even then she couldn't see who it was. "There are guards outside." She balled her hand into a fist, refusing to allow her voice to quiver. "I could scream."

"There's only the guard at the gate, and he's too far away. I had to hurt the others. Sometimes you have to hurt when you love."

She gauged the distance to the front door. "How did you get in?"

"Over the wall by the tennis courts. You haven't been using the tennis courts. I've been watching for you."

"The alarm —"

"I took care of the alarm. I have some knowledge. My reputation for careful research is well deserved." Brewster stepped out of the shadows with the music box in his hands.

"James." The air in the poolhouse was sultry, but Chantel began to shiver. "Why are you doing this?"

"I love you." His eyes were glazed, and she could see no emotion in them as he walked closer. "When you first formed in my mind, I knew I had to have you. Then you were there, flesh, blood. Real. I had this made for you."

He held out the music box, and Chantel stepped back.

"Don't be afraid of me, Hailey."

"James, I'm Chantel. Chantel."

"Yes, yes, of course." He smiled at her, then set the box down on a little table beside the tub. It continued to play, romantic and sweet. "Chantel O'Hurley, with the perfect face. I've dreamed of you for months. I can't write. My wife thinks I'm agonizing over my new book. But there is no book. There'll never be another book. Chantel, you wouldn't keep my flowers."

"I'm sorry." Quinn would be back, she told herself. The nightmare would be over. She felt exposed in her brief suit, so she reached for her wrap. Training kept her gestures casual, even as her heart roared in her head. "It was the way you sent them, James. You frightened me."

"I never meant to. Hailey —"

"Chantel," she corrected, a flutter of panic in her voice. "I'm Chantel. James, I think we should go into the house and talk about this."

"Chantel?" He looked momentarily puzzled. "No, no, I want to be alone with you. I've waited too long for tonight. The perfect night, when the moon is full. The song." He looked at the music box. "It was meant for you."

"Why didn't you just talk to me?"

"You would have rejected me. Rejected me," he repeated in a rising voice. "Do you think I'm a fool? I've seen you with those young men, all muscles and smooth faces. But none of them love you like I do. You've driven me mad with waiting. You were obsessed with Brad. It was always Brad."

"There is no Brad!" she shouted. "He's a character. There is no Hailey. You made them up. They're not real."

"You're real. I've seen you with him. I've watched the way you look at him, let him touch you, when it should be me. But I've been patient. Tonight." He started toward her. "I've waited for tonight."

Chantel raced for the front door, knowing that if she could beat him she'd have a chance. Grabbing the knob, she pulled, but it held firm.

"I locked it from the outside," Brewster told her quietly. "I knew you'd try to run away. I knew you'd throw my love back in my face."

Chantel spun around, pressing her back to the door. "You don't love me. You're confused. I'm an actress. I'm not your Hailey."

He winced as if in pain and pressed his fingers to his eyes. "Such headaches," he murmured. "No, don't," he warned when she edged toward the back door. He blocked her way, then stepped back into the shadows to pick something up. "I know what I have to do, and there's no running for either of us now, Hailey."

"I'm not —"

"It's too late," he said viciously. "Too late. I guess I've always known. I hate what you've done to me." He pressed his fingers to his temple as tears welled up in his eyes. "But as God is my witness, I can't let another man have you. You're mine. From the first moment, you were mine. If you could only understand that."

"James." She was afraid to touch him, but she took a small step closer. "Please, come into the house with me. I'm — I'm cold," she said quickly. "I'm wet. I need to change. Then we can sit down and talk."

He looked at her, but saw only what he wanted to see. "You can't lie to me. I created you. You're going to try to leave. You want to see them put me away. My doctor wants to put me away, but I know what I have to do. For both of us. It ends here, Hailey."

He held up the can, and she smelled the gasoline. "Oh, God, no."

"You were meant to die in the fire before, but I couldn't do it then. Now I have to."

He turned the can over as she lunged at him. It hit the floor with a clatter, then skidded, gas soaking into the wood. She fought to get past him. Chantel heard him sob as he shoved her down and her head hit the table. Suddenly there were shooting stars in front of her eyes.

"Chantel's going to want to open a bottle of champagne."

"I think we could all use it," Matt commented as they walked into the house. "Quinn, I'd appreciate it if you'd let me tell her."

"You're entitled." He looked around the cool, quiet hall. "You were entitled to take a swing at me back there."

"You're bigger than I am," Matt said easily.

"I overreacted, Matt. I'm not used to that." He thought about Chantel waiting for him upstairs, and what he would have done, would continue to do to keep her safe. "The thing is I jumped on you with both feet because it was the first solid lead I've had in this whole mess."

"From what you told me, it looks like everything the florist told you fit me."

"What fits you fits someone else. I'm missing it," Quinn murmured. "I'm missing it because I'm too close. You know what the first rule of law enforcement, private or public service, is? Don't get involved."

"A little late for that I take it."

"Way too late. She believed in you," he added. "I think you should know that. Even after I spelled it all out for her she stood behind you."

Touched, Matt fiddled with the lapel of his jacket. "She's a very special woman."

"She's the most beautiful woman I've ever met, inside and out. Integrity. You don't see the integrity when you look at her, or the guts, or the loyalty. It's taken me awhile to get under the surface and see all there is to her." He moved his shoulders, restless, dissatisfied. "Maybe if I'd had a little more of her faith in the people she cares for, I wouldn't have chased down a blind alley."

Matt followed Quinn's gaze up the stairs. If Quinn had overreacted, he thought, then he himself had underreacted. The past few weeks he'd been too involved with his own world to give one of his closest friends the kind of time and attention she needed. He turned the bottle in his hand. He was going to start making up for it now.

"Look, I was pretty steamed before, but I think you're as crazy about Chantel as I am about Marion. I probably would have done the same thing myself."

"Maybe." Quinn glanced at the stairs again. He didn't want champagne. He only wanted to be alone with Chantel, but she needed to see Matt, needed to talk to him. She'd be relieved, and yet he wondered if she would feel the same frustration he was experiencing. They'd come so far, yet they'd gone nowhere. "I hate what she's going through."

"So do I." Matt laid a hand on his shoulder. "The past couple months have taught me that love can drive anybody crazy. I guess it's like Brewster said in that interview."

"What interview?"

"It was in the paper tonight. They did an article on *Strangers*, focusing on Hailey. The way he described her, hell, you'd have thought she was real. But he said something that rang true — about how when a man really loves a woman, he sees her as no one else does, that no matter what he accomplishes, what he fails at, she stays at the center of his life, rules it just by being. I guess I was feeling sentimental when I read it," Matt said with a trace of embarrassment. "But I thought I knew what he meant. He even got Chantel and Hailey's names mixed up once."

"What?"

"You could tell the reporter got a charge out of that. He played up how Chantel must be turning in an Emmy-winning performance to have the writer confuse the actress with the character."

"Damn." Quinn slammed his fist against the newel post and started up the stairs. "He practically confessed this afternoon. He all but spit it in my lap."

"What are you —" But Quinn was gone. Matt just shrugged and wondered if he had time to telephone Marion.

"Call the fire department!" Quinn shouted, taking the steps three at a time. "The poolhouse is going up."

"It's on fire?"

"She's in there." Quinn was at the door before Matt picked up the phone. "He's got her in there."

Chantel shook her head to try to clear it. The room swam, and she struggled to her hands and knees. She smelled the smoke first, thick and pungent, as it had been that afternoon during the filming. But this wasn't special effects, she remembered. She heard the crackle of flames and looked over to see the floor turn to fire.

He was still blocking the back door, standing there as if hypnotized by the fire, which was spreading fast. He wasn't trying to leave. He would die here, he wanted to die here. And he would take her with him.

Chantel stood, choking on smoke as she looked around frantically. Her head throbbed and spun, but she couldn't allow herself the luxury of passing out. The windows were too high. She'd never get out that way. The front door was barred. There was only one exit. She had to get past him before the fire closed it off.

Her breath came in a fit of coughing, but

he didn't hear. The flames held his attention as they ate greedily at the far wall. The heat was growing, visible in waves that shimmered between her and the door. Moving fast, Chantel grabbed a towel and dumped it in the tub. Then, draping it over her face, she looked for a weapon.

The music box sat on the table, playing though the tune was muffled by the sound of flames. She took it and, on legs that threatened to buckle, walked behind Brewster.

He was crying. She heard it now as she raised the heavy wooden box over her head. Tears were streaking her own face, blurring her vision. It was so much like the scene she had studied, rehearsed, tried to understand.

Hailey, she thought as smoke clouded her brain. It was the cabin, her New England retreat. She was Hailey and she'd brought tragedy on herself, on those who had loved her. Past mistakes, past loves, past lives. If only she hadn't given her love and her innocence to Brad. . . . To Dustin?

Her vision went gray, and she fought to clear it. There was no Brad. Only Quinn. Quinn was real and she was Chantel. An O'Hurley. O'Hurleys were survivors.

Weeping, she smashed the box down on Brewster's head.

When he crumpled at her feet, she could

only crouch, panting, struggling to find air in a room consumed by smoke and flame.

Had she killed him? She looked at the doorway, framed now by flames. Her only way out. Survival. She took a step forward, stopped, then bent over Brewster.

He'd loved her. Mad or sane, whatever he'd done had been tied to her. Somehow, later, she would sort it out, but she couldn't save herself without trying to save him.

She snatched off the towel and covered his face with it. The ceiling gave an ominous crack, but she didn't dare look. She didn't think. Everything was centered on living. Hooking her hands under his armpits, Chantel began to drag him toward the door and closer to the flames.

She was losing. There was no air to fill her lungs as she dragged the deadweight of Brewster's unconscious body. The fire was winning, edging closer. She felt the furnace blast of heat on her skin and wished desperately that she'd taken the time to wet some towels.

Inches from the door, she stumbled and fell, lightheaded from lack of oxygen. A little farther, she demanded, dragging herself and Brewster across the floor. Oh, God, just a little farther.

She watched, too dazed to be frightened,

as a beam fell, flaming, into the hot tub.

"Chantel!"

She heard the shout dimly as her consciousness started to waver. Somehow she managed to gain another two inches.

Quinn kicked in the front door and saw nothing but a wall of flame. He screamed for her again and heard nothing but fire. The roof was going. He ran for the doorway, but the heat drove him back. It was then he saw her or thought he did, slumped by the far wall, with the flames separating them.

Coughing on the smoke he'd swallowed, he raced around the building, praying for the first time in his adult life.

She'd almost made it. That was his first thought as he saw her, collapsed against Brewster near the door. Burning wood showered from the ceiling as he hurled his body over hers. He felt it hit and sear his hand before he dragged her out onto the grass.

"In the name of God —" Matt began as he raced to them.

"Brewster's in there," Quinn managed. "Take care of her."

Quinn fought the heat again, nearly giving way at what had been the back doorway. Crawling on his belly, he inched closer, until he managed to grip Brewster's wrist. If there was a pulse, he couldn't feel it, but he dragged him back. As the roof collapsed inward, he left Brewster lying on the grass and rolled onto his back to draw in air.

"Chantel." Still coughing, he crawled to her. Her face was smeared with soot. He heard the sirens as she opened her eyes to look at him.

"Quinn. He —"

"I got him out. Don't try to talk now." She began to shiver, though the heat was still intense. Quinn stripped off his shirt and covered her. "She's in shock," he said tersely. "Smoke inhalation. She needs the hospital."

"I told them to send an ambulance." Matt peeled off his sweater and added it to Quinn's shirt. "She's going to be all right. She's tough."

"Yeah." Quinn cradled her head in his lap. "Yeah."

"He thought I was Hailey." She groped for his hand as she wavered in and out of consciousness.

"I know. Shhh." He took her hand and squeezed. The pain from his burns was real. She was real. And they were alive.

"I . . . for a little while in there, so did I. Quinn, tell me who I am."

"Chantel O'Hurley. The only woman I've ever loved."

"Thanks," she whispered, and drifted off.

By the time he was allowed to see her, Quinn had gone twenty-four hours without sleep. He'd refused to leave the hospital to change, and his clothes were streaked and reeking of smoke. Throughout the night he'd paced the halls and driven the nurses crazy.

She'd been treated for shock and smoke inhalation. The doctors had assured him that all she needed was rest. He intended to see and speak to her himself before he went anywhere. And when he went, she was going with him.

At dawn the day after the fire, Chantel awoke from a drugged sleep. When the doctor came out of her room, he was shaking his head. He looked at Quinn, noting his bandaged hand and singed clothing. "You can see her now. I'm going to process her discharge papers, though if you have any influence you should talk her into staying one more day for observation."

"I can take care of her at home."

The doctor sent a dubious look in the direction of the door. "Maybe you can. Mr. Doran?"

Quinn stopped with his hand on the knob. "Yes?"

"She's a very strong-willed woman."

"I know." For the first time in hours, Quinn smiled. He opened the door to see Chantel sitting up in bed, frowning into a mirror.

"I look horrible."

"Beauty's only skin deep," he said as she lowered the mirror to look at him.

"It's a good thing, because you look worse than I do. Oh, Quinn . . ." She spread her arms wide. "You're really here," she whispered as she used all her strength to squeeze. "It's all right now, isn't it? Everything's going to be all right."

"It's over. I should have taken better care of you."

"I'll dock your pay."

"Damn it, Chantel, it's not a joke."

"You saved my life," she told him as she drew away.

"When I think of what might have happened —"

"No." She put her fingertips to his mouth. "I don't want to think of 'what ifs' anymore, Quinn. I'm safe and so are you. That's all that matters now. And . . . and James . . ."

"He'll live," Quinn said, answering her unspoken question. He stood and began to prowl the room. "He's going to be put away, Chantel. I'm going to help see to that."

"Quinn, he was so pathetic, so confused. He created something that overwhelmed him."

"He would have killed you."

"He would have killed Hailey," she corrected. "I can only pity him."

"Forget him," Quinn told her, knowing he would have to if he didn't want to be eaten alive by bitterness. "Your family's coming."

"Here? All of them?"

"Your sisters, your parents. Nobody knows how to reach Trace."

"Quinn, I don't want to disrupt Maddy's honeymoon. And everyone else —"

"Wants to make sure you're all right. That's what families are for, right?"

"Yes." She folded her hands. "It is. Quinn, you deserve a family, your own family."

He turned to her, ready to fight for what he needed. "I know what I want, Chantel."

"Yes, I think you do." She'd made her decision when she'd opened her eyes on the grass and seen his face. "Quinn, before all of this happened last night, I was waiting for you. I knew when you came back and held me I'd make the right choice, for both of us." She glanced around the room, then into the mirror. With a grimace she set it facedown on the table beside her. "This isn't exactly how I expected things to be, but it would help a lot if you'd come here and put your arms around me."

He sat on the bed beside her and gathered her close. "Listen, I have to tell you this. When I got there last night and the poolhouse was burning, I knew you were inside because my heart had stopped. If I had lost you, it would never have started again."

"Quinn." She lifted her head, searching for his lips. Finding them, she found all the answers she needed. "I'd like a short engagement," she said, smiling. "Very, very short."